D1353070

# RED HANDED

An anthology of
radical crime stories

Edited and introduced by
*Jon E. Lewis*

**Allison & Busby**
Published by W. H. Allen & Co Plc

An Allison & Busby book
Published in 1989 by
W. H. Allen & Co Plc
Sekforde House
175/9 St John St
London EC1V 4LL

Copyright © 1989 Jon E. Lewis

Phototypeset by Input Typesetting Ltd, London
Printed in Great Britain by
Courier International Ltd, Tiptree, Essex

ISBN 0 85031 995 1 HB
0 74900 075 9 PB

# CONTENTS

# CONTENTS

# Acknowledgements

Many people gave help and advice in the preparation of this book. Accordingly, I wish to express my gratitude to: Clive Allison, Betty Clary, Andy Croft, the librarians of the Institute of Latin American Studies, Antonia McMeeking, my parents, John and Tereza Roberts, Marilyn and Norman Schwenk, Amelia S. Simpson, Joan Stempel, Tony Williams and, most of all, Penny Stempel.

# Acknowledgements

'Tang' by Chester Himes. Reprinted from *Black on Black*, published by Michael Joseph. Copyright © 1967 Chester Himes, Reproduced by kind permission of Lesley Himes.

'Hot as a Pistol' by Karen Wilson. Reprinted from *The Woman Sleuth Anthology*, published by the Crossing Press. Copyright © 1988 Karen Wilson. Reproduced by kind permission of the author and Irene Zahava.

'The Barber Has Killed His Wife' by Albert Cossery. Reprinted from *Modern Reading*, No. 13, 1945. Copyright © 1945 Albert Cossery. Reproduced by kind permission of the author.

'The Best Chess Player in the World' by Julian Symons. Reprinted from *The Tigers of Subtopia*, published by Macmillan. Copyright © 1982 Julian Symons. Reproduced by kind permission of Curtis Brown Ltd. and the author.

'I Spy' by Joan Smith. Copyright © Joan Smith.

'The Collector' by Rubem Fonseca. Copyright © 1965 Rubem Fonseca. Reprinted from *O Cobrador*, Nova Fronteira. Reproduced by kind permission of Agencia Literaria Carmen Balcells. Translation copyright © 1989 Penarth Translation Agency.

'If I Quench Thee . . .' by William E. Chambers. Reprinted from *The Mystery Writers' Choice 1977* by Gollancz. Copyright © 1977 William E. Chambers. Reproduced by kind permission of the author.

'The Flaw in the System' by Jim Thompson. Copyright © 1957 Jim

## ACKNOWLEDGEMENTS

Thompson. Reprinted from *Ellery Queen's Mystery Magazine* 1957.
Reproduced by kind permission of John Farquharson Ltd and
Alberta Thompson.

'The Five Pin Stands Alone' by Gordon DeMarco. Copyright ©
1989 Gordon DeMarco.

# INTRODUCTION

The verdict of history on the crime genre is likely to be that it was a nasty case of Snobbery with Violence. After all, what is it mostly but tales of gentlemen detectives and police officers upholding the rule of law and order?

Or, to put it another way, most fictional crime is about the Establishment defending society as it is. Even as a passionate devotee of the crime story, I am forced to confess that it is a peculiarly genteel and conservative form of literature.

But there is an alternative tradition of crime fiction to be found. One which uses the crime story not as a blunt instrument of reaction, but as a means of probing and exposing the injustices of society. A minor tradition certainly, but also the oldest there is. Because the first crime story proper was not written, as often supposed, by the conservative Edgar Allan Poe, but by the anarchist, William Godwin.

Published in 1794, *Caleb Williams* is the account of a murder, and its detection by the clerk who is the book's hero. But *Caleb Williams* is much more than an entertainment. It is also a radical political critique of a society where despotism reigns, and where the law is biased in favour of the rich and powerful. (As anybody who reads Godwin's novel will not be surprised to find, it was originally entitled *Things As They Are*.)

After Godwin, however, and some early crime stories which showed a distinct sympathy with the criminal, the direction of the genre was steadily to the Right. The nadir was reached in England during the years between the World Wars – the so-called 'Golden Age' of crime fiction.

It is not that the classical detective stories of Christie,

Sayers, Allingham & Co. are not enjoyable as puzzles. It is that the social functions they perform are reactionary. Namely, to reassure those with a stake in the existing social system that it will last forever – and to guide the readers' behaviour to ensure that it does.

(It is thus no accident that the whodunnit's Great Detective always triumphs over those who threaten to upset the prevailing order. Or that the whodunnit either ignores, or stigmatises, anybody who is not Anglo-Saxon, right-wing, heterosexual, upper-class and patriarchal. Or that it is so strongly on the side of the law, the first refuge of the propertied and the privileged.)

Of course, the whodunnit is not unique in these respects. Probably two thirds of the crime stories written have been similarly guilty of attempting to perpetuate the status quo. It is just that the whodunnit is a particularly extreme and influential example.

Although some exceptions to the rule of reaction were offered by the stories of progressives who dabbled in the crime form, it was not until the late 1920s in America that Godwinian principles were truly revived in the genre – with the creation of 'hardboiled' crime fiction by Dashiell Hammett.

A central concern of Hammett's works (the finest of which is the 1929 novel *Red Harvest*) is the civic corruption which grew up in the wake of Prohibition. As Hammett revealed, corruption had become all-pervasive. The gangsters owned the cops and ran City Hall, while the difference between gangsterism and 'legitimate' capitalism was virtually zero – about the width of a nickel.

In such a world the only guarantor of justice was the shamus or private eye. Since, unlike other detectives (fictional and real) he was not of the upper classes or of the state machine. On the contrary, Hammett's Continental Op (later Sam Spade) was a proletarian man, and the tough-guy values he embodied were those of blue-collar workers (and readers) in an age of adversity. And the language he spoke was the democratic vernacular of the American people.

Hammett was not the only member of the hardboiled school who was a social critic (although he was the most left-wing), and many of his successors – like Ross Macdonald and Jim Thompson – continued to use the crime story as a social scalpel. Indeed, of all the variants of fictional crime, the hardboiled has been the most inclined to radicalism. Although, it must be stressed, it has been a radicalism which has more or less exclusively concerned itself with the *class* assumption of crime fiction, and has ignored (at best) those of race, gender etc.

In Britain, the other major centre of crime fiction production, radicalism did not reappear until the very end of the 1930s, when the spy story, a sub-genre previously totally infected with 'Sapper'-style xenophobia, was given a necessary dose of leftist anti-fascism by Eric Ambler. And it has only been in the most recent decades that the conservative stranglehold over British crime fiction as a whole has shown any perceptible signs of weakening.

A similar loss of conservative grip has occurred in other countries too during this period. One cause of this has been the impact of the post-war social liberation movements on the genre. One result has been a relative decline in English-style murder stories. Another is that it is now possible to find women in crime who are something other than femmes fatales, products of male wish-fulfilment or posh silver-haired old ladies. Women like Vic Warshawski, Kate Fanzler and Kate Baeier in the stories of, respectively, Sara Paretsky, Amanda Cross and Gillian Slovo.

And lesbians and gays who are something other than figures of fun. For instance, Dave Brandsetter in the novels of Joseph Hansen and Emma Victor in those of Mary Wings. (Not to mention bisexuals like Duffy in the stories of Dan Kavanagh.)

And ever since Chester Himes began writing his Harlem police novels in the late 1950s, it has been possible to find blacks who are something other than Uncle Toms and Uppity Niggers.

Unfortunately, none of the above should be exaggerated.

The crime story still has a depressing tendency towards gentility and prejudice. (A tendency likely to become strengthened by the political climate in some countries of the Northern hemisphere.) Which is why anybody of a progressive outlook, or anybody wanting a change from the usual genre product, will, I believe, find the following ten stories to their taste.

This anthology is not a representative selection of the historical and international breadth of radical crime fiction. Not least because such a thing would be impossible in a book this size. But also because it seemed best to me to include only complete pieces of fiction. And several of the most important radical crime writers, notably the Swedish team of Maj Sjowall and Per Wahloo, have not (unfortunately) indulged in the short story form.

Yet there are stories here from Brazil, Britain, Egypt and the USA. There are stories as diverse in type as the spy and the private eye, as well as one which might be termed a philosophical 'whydunnit' (that by Albert Cossery). The oldest story is Jack London's, first published in 1913, and there are two stories which have never been published before, those by Gordon DeMarco and Joan Smith. And one which has never been published in English before – that by Fonseca. Some of the authors are great names, others talented newcomers.

The radicalism of the stories ranges from those which simply insert as the good guys those who are always the bad guys in crime, to stories written from black power and marxist viewpoints. Few of the stories are what is sometimes called 'ideologically sound'. But all of them are unusual and excellent pieces of crime writing (Does it need to be said that a crime story which is a failure as an entertainment will be useless in persuading the reader of its message?) And all of the stories ask: What really is the crime? Who really dunnit. The sort of questions that Godwin and Hammett asked.

And it is to these two crime writers and fighters for social justice that the book is dedicated. I hope it is a worthy tribute to them.

# TANG

## Chester Himes

*Chester Himes was born into a middle-class family in Missouri in 1909. He began writing while serving a seven year prison sentence for burglary, and with the publication of* If He Hollers Let Him Go *(1945) was established as the leading Black Protest novelist of his generation. In 1953 he emigrated to Europe, where crime fiction (notably the series of police novels featuring Coffin Ed Johnson and Grave Digger Jones) moved to the centre of his literary activity. Chester Himes died in Spain in 1984.*

*The short story 'Tang' was written in 1967 when, in Himes's own words, 'my thoughts had concentrated on BLACK REVOLUTION'.*

A man called T-bone Smith sat in a cold-water slum flat on 113th Street east of Eighth Avenue in Harlem, looking at television with his old lady, Tang. They had a television set but they didn't have anything to eat. It was after ten o'clock at night and the stores were closed, but that didn't make any difference because they didn't have any money. It was a two-roomed flat so the television was in the kitchen with the table and the stove. Because it was summertime, the stove was cold and the windows were open.

T-bone was clad only in a pair of greasy black pants and his bare back torso was ropy with lean hard muscles and decorated with an elaborate variety of scars. His long narrow face was hinged on a mouth with lips the size of automobile tires and the corners of his sloe-shaped eyes were sticky with matter. The short hard burrs on his watermelon head were the color of half-burnt ashes. He had his bare black feet propped up on the kitchen table with the white soles towards

1

the television screen. He was white-mouthed from hunger but was laughing like an idiot at two blackfaced white minstrels on the television screen who earned more money every week by blackening their faces and acting foolish than T-bone had earned in all his life.

In between laughing he was trying to get his old lady, Tang, to go down into Central Park and trick with some white man so they could eat.

'Go on, baby, you can be back in an hour with 'nuff bread so we can scoff.'

'I'se tired as you are,' she said evilly. 'Go sell yo' own ass to whitey, you luvs him so much.'

She had once been a beautiful jet-black woman with a broad flat face and softly rounded features which looked as though they had been made by a child at play; her fingers had been something to invoke instant visions of sex contortions and black ecstasy. But both face and figure had been corroded by vice and hunger and now she was a lean, angular crone with burnt red hair and flat black features which looked like they had been molded by a stamping machine. Only her eyes looked alive; they were red, mean, disillusioned and defiant. She was clad in a faded green mother hubbard which looked as though it had never been laundered and her big, buniony feet trod restlessly about the dirty, rotting kitchen linoleum. The soles were unseen but the tops had wrinkled black skin streaked with dirt.

Suddenly above the sound of the gibbering of the blackface white minstrels, they heard an impatient hammering on the door. Both knew instantly someone had first tried the doorbell, which had never worked. They looked suspiciously at one another. Neither could imagine anyone it could be except the police, so they quickly scanned the room to see if there were any incriminating evidence in sight; although, aside from her hustling about the lagoon in Central Park, neither had committed any crime recently enough to interest the police. Finally she stuck her bare feet into some old felt slippers and rubbed red lipstick over her rusty lips while he got up and shambled across the floor in his bare feet to open the door.

A young black uniformed messenger with smooth skin and bright intelligent eyes asked, 'Mister Smith?'

'Dass me,' T-bone admitted.

The messenger extended a long cardboard box wrapped in white paper and tied with a red ribbon. Conspicuous on the white wrapping paper was the green and white label of a florist, decorated with pink and yellow flowers and on the lines for the name and address were the typed words: *Mr T. Smith, West 113th Street, 4th floor,* The messenger placed the box directly into T-bone's outstretched hands and waited until T-bone had a firm grip before releasing it.

'Flowers for you, sir,' he trilled.

T-bone was so startled he almost let go of the box, but the messenger was already hurtling down the stairs, and T-bone was too slow-witted to react in any fashion. He simply stood there holding the box in his outstretched hands, his mouth hanging open, not a thought in his head; he just looked stupid and stunned.

But Tang's thoughts were working like a Black IBM. 'Who sending you flowers, black and ugly as you is?' she demanded suspiciously from across the room. And the fact of it was, she really meant it. Still he was her man, simple-minded or not, and it made her jealous for him to get flowers, other than for his funeral, which hadn't happened yet.

'Dese ain't flowers,' he said, sounding just as suspicious as she had. 'Lessen they be flowers of lead.'

'Maybe it's some scoff from the government's thing for the poor folks,' she perked hopefully.

'Not unless it's pig-iron knuckles,' he said.

She bent over beside him and gingerly fingered the white wrapped box. 'It's got your name on it,' she said. 'And your address. What would anybody be sending to your name and your address?'

'We gonna soon see,' he said and stepped across the room to lay the box on the table. It made a clunking sound. The two blackfaced comedians danced merrily on the television

3

screen until interrupted by a beautiful blonde reading a commercial for Nucream, which made dirty skin so fresh and white.

She stood back and watched him break the ribbon and tear off the white wrapping paper. She was practically holding her breath when he opened the gray cardboard carton, but he was too unimaginative to have any thoughts one way or another. If God had sent him down a trunk full of gold bricks from heaven he would have wondered if he was expected to brick up a wall which wasn't his.

Inside the cardboard box they saw a long object wrapped in brown oiled paper and packed in paper excelsior in the way they had seen machine tools packed when they had worked in a shipyard in Newark before she had listened to his sweet talk and had come to Harlem to be his whore. She couldn't imagine anybody sending him a machine tool unless he had been engaged in activities which she didn't know anything about. Which wasn't likely, she thought, as long as she made enough to feed him. He just stared at it stupidly, wondering why anybody would send him something which looked like something he couldn't use even if he wanted to use it.

'Pick it up,' she said sharply. 'It ain't gonna bite you.'

'I ain't scaird of nuttin bitin' me,' he said fearlessly lifting the object from its bed of excelsior. 'It ain't heavy as I thought,' he said stupidly, although he had given no indication of what he had thought.

She noticed a typewritten sheet which had been lying underneath the object which she instantly suspected was a letter. Quickly she snatched it up.

'Wuss dat?' he asked with the automatic suspicion of one who can't read.

She knew he couldn't read and instinctive jealousy provoked her to needle him. 'Writing! That's what.'

'What's it say?' he demanded, panic-stricken.

First she read the typed words to herself: *WARNING!!! DO NOT INFORM POLICE!!! LEARN YOUR WEAPON AND WAIT FOR INSTRUCTIONS!!! REPEAT!!! LEARN YOUR*

4

*WEAPON AND WAIT FOR INSTRUCTIONS!!! WARNING!!!
DO NOT INFORM POLICE!!! FREEDOM IS NEAR!!!*
Then she read them aloud. They alarmed him so much
that sweat broke out over his face and his eyes stretched until
they were completely round. Frantically he began tearing off
the oiled wrapping paper. The dull gleam of an automatic
rifle came into sight. She gasped. She had never seen a rifle
that looked as dangerous as that. But he had seen and handled the M-14 used by the United States Army when he had
served in the Korean war.

'Iss a M-14,' he said. 'Iss uh army gun.'

He was terrified. His skin dried and appeared dusty.

'I done served my time,' he continued, adding, 'Efen iss
stolen I don't want it. Wuss anybody wanna send me a stolen
gun for?'

Her eyes blazed in a face contorted with excitement. 'It's
the uprising, nigger!' she cried. 'We gonna be free!'

'Uprising?' He shied away from the thought as though it
were a rattlesnake. *'Free?'* He jumped as though the snake
had bit him. 'Ise already free. All someun wants to do is get
my ass in jail.' He held the rifle as though it were a bomb
which might go off in his hand.

But she looked at the gun with awe and love. 'That'll chop
a white policeman two ways sides and flat. That'll blow the
shit out of whitey's asshole.'

'Wut?' He put the gun down onto the table and pushed it
away from him. 'Shoot the white police? Someun 'spects me
tuh shoot de white police?'

'Why not? You wanna uprise, don't you?'

'Uprise? Whore, is you crazy? Uprise where?'

'Uprise here, nigger. Is you that stupid? Here we is and
here we is gonna uprise.'

'Not me! I ain't gonna get my ass blown off waving that
thing around. We had them things in Korea and them cats
kilt us niggers like flies.'

'You got shit in your blood,' she said contemptuously. 'Let
me feel that thing.'

She picked up the rifle from the table and held it as though

5

she were shooting rabbits about the room. 'Baby,' she said directly to the gun. 'You and me can make it, baby.'

'Wuss de matter wid you? You crazy?' he shouted. 'Put that thing down. I'm gonna go tell de man 'fo we gets both our ass in jail.'

'You going to tell whitey?' she asked in surprise. 'You going run tell the man 'bout this secret that'll make us free?'

'Shut yo' mouth, whore, Ise doin it much for you as I is for me.'

At first she didn't take him seriously. 'For me, nigger? You think I wanna sell my pussy to whitey all my life?' But, with the gun in her hand, the question was rhetorical. She kept shooting at imaginary rabbits about the room, thinking she could go hunting and kill her a whitey or two. Hell, give her enough time and bullets she could kill them all.

Her words caused him to frown in bewilderment. 'You wanna stop being a whore, whore?' he asked in amazement. 'Hell, whore, we gotta live.'

'You call this living?' She drew the gun tight to her breast as though it were a lover. 'This the only thing what made me feel alive since I met you.'

He looked outraged. 'You been lissenin to that black power shit, them Black Panthers 'n that shit,' he accused. 'Ain't I always done what's best?'

'Yeah, put me on the block to sell my black pussy to poor white trash.'

'I ain' gonna argy wid you,' he said in exasperation. 'Ise goan'n get de cops 'fore we both winds up daid.'

Slowly and deliberately, she aimed the gun at him. 'You call whitey and I'll waste you,' she threatened.

He was moving toward the door but the sound of her voice stopped him. He turned about and looked at her. It was more the sight of her than the meaning of her words which made him hesitate. He wasn't a man to dare anyone and she had sounded as though she would blow him away. But he knew she was tender-hearted and wouldn't hurt him as long as he didn't cross her. So he decided to kid her along until he could grab the gun, then he'd whip her ass. With this in

6

mind he began shuffling around the table in her direction, grinning obsequiously, playing the part of the forgiving lover. 'Baby, I were jes playing – '

'Maybe you are but I ain't,' she warned him.

'I weren't gonna call the cops, I were jes gonna see if the door is locked.'

'You see and you won't know it.'

She talking too much, he thought, shuffling closer to her. Suddenly he grabbed for the gun. She pulled the trigger. Nothing happened. Both froze in shock. It had never occurred to either that the gun was not loaded.

He was the first to react. He burst out laughing. 'Haw-haw-haw.'

'Wouldn't have been so funny if this thing had been loaded,' she said sourly.

Suddenly his face contorted with rage. It was as though the relief felt by the dissipation of his fear had been replaced by fury. He whipped out a springblade knife. 'I teach you, whore,' he raved. 'You try to kill me.'

She looked from the knife to his face and said stoically, 'I shoulda known, you are whitey's slave; you'll never be free.'

'Free of you,' he shouted and began slashing at her.

She tried to protect herself with the rifle but shortly he had cut it out of her grasp. She backed around the table trying to keep away from the slashing blade. But soon the blade began reaching her flesh and the floor became covered with blood; she crumpled and fell and died, as she had known she would after the first look at his enraged face.

7

# HOT AS A PISTOL

## Karen Wilson

*Karen Wilson (1952– ) lives in Los Angeles, where she works as a technical writer by day and a short story writer by night.*

*'Hot as a Pistol' features lesbian private eye Wiggins and is set in Southern California (A locale which used to be the exclusive preserve of the male tough-guy PI of the Marlowe type.) The story was first published in 1988.*

The ringing phone saved me from the clutches of humidity-induced catatonia. The voice on the other end rescued me from the tedium of scaring up another counterfeit jeans case. As the ceiling fan in the outer office turned hopelessly, my young detecting career moved beyond the bread-and-butter stage. I had my first real caper, as Uncle Raymond would have said.

Beverly Grayson gave me the particulars with just a touch of panic in her voice. Wanda James, her business partner, had missed an appointment a few hours earlier and her house seemed 'funny'. Ransacked? No. Forced entry? No. Just funny, like what's wrong with this picture. Could she prevail upon my professional expertise for advice on what to do next?

I had a serious case of the curiosities for Beverly and she knew it. We had met for drinks a few times and had worked all the way up to overt flirtation. Beverly had an anachronistic air about her, one that said 'good breeding'. She held herself tall and straight, creating the illusion of modelesque dimensions. In reality, she stood a shade under five feet, six inches and was much too well-endowed for the current fashions.

Her blond hair grew thick and just beyond her shoulders. She pushed it back from her face frequently with a slender, manicured hand. Beverly's blue eyes changed from sparkling to smoldering to stone-cold, depending on her mood. I preferred the smoldering mood myself. Then, her demeanor softened and the promise of her full lips was unmistakable.

Beverly had introduced me to Wanda on our second Happy Hour date. The bar happened to be close to their casting agency, and Wanda happened to drop by after working a little later than everyone else. Wanda, a few years older than Beverly, was quick with a smile. As aloof as Beverly seemed, Wanda came off as your best friend for years now. The way she looked me up and down and over without missing a beat in the conversation also told me Wanda was a friendly woman, very friendly.

As soon as Beverly mentioned I was a detective – 'a female Magnum' is how she put it – Wanda launched into a long story about mysterious phone calls at three a.m., shadows around her house, and a spine-tingling close call on the canyon roads. And the punch line was that she, Wanda had been on the receiving end of these spookies for a couple of weeks now.

Who was behind it all? She didn't know. Who did she think was behind it? She couldn't imagine. Had she called the police? Once; they said they'd rather wait to get involved. Wait? Until something happened. Did she feel like something was going to happen? Maybe. Did she want a private investigator? Maybe, she'd call me. I gave Wanda my card and Beverly gave me a smile.

A week later, Beverly hired me to find Wanda James.

The Civic Center high that day was ninety-eight and the humidity stayed around eighty percent. What had happened to Southern California's perfect weather? Why live in LA when it feels like New York without the museums? Had Beverly sounded too upset to be interested in dinner? Just what were the ethics of personal involvements with clients? I couldn't remember Sam Spade passing up the company of a beautiful woman just because he worked for her. And none

10

of Uncle Raymond's old pals had mentioned any special restrictions for lesbian detectives. Precedent was on my side.

Driving west on Melrose, then Sunset into the afternoon sun, I let my heat-dulled brain wander about those sundry tracks. How to turn drinks into dinner and dinner into a weekend away constituted the most consistent train of thought I had on the way to meet with Beverly at Wanda's Laurel Canyon home.

About twenty minutes after her call, I parked the loaner car I'd been using for a week in the driveway of a square Spanish-style stucco abode. The house, with its red tile roof, sat flush against the canyon wall in the Hollywood Hills. And Beverly's white Mercedes sat in the carport, top down. I could just see her driving up the Coast Highway at sunset, blond hair swept back in the wind, too cool. I put on my linen jacket and felt too hot.

'Nice hat.' Beverly complimented my broad-brim straw number as she let me in.

She calmly offered me a cold drink and led the way to a canvas-covered deck on the north side of the house.

'The air conditioning seems to have been off for hours,' she explained. 'It's actually cooler out here since the house was all closed up.'

We sat in cushioned wicker chairs, sipping gin and tonic, evoking images of memsahibs waiting for the cricket match to resume. It could have been our white ensembles – hers of silk – which put me in mind of colonial India. I continued to lose the here-and-now as Beverly's thick blonde hair fell across her left eye when she moved to set her drink on the table between us. Suddenly I was transported to a Veronica Lake movie. Did that make me Alan Ladd? The fact that he was a bad guy in that movie and I'm hardly ever a bad guy got me back to the present. That and Beverly's questions.

'Do you think I should be worried? What do you think could have happened to her? Did you believe that story of hers, you know, about someone calling and threatening her?' Beverly rushed her words despite an obvious effort to sound in charge.

'Don't worry until there's some reason. That's my motto,' I reassured her.

'It's just not like her to not show up. And her car's gone. So she went *somewhere*.' Beads of perspiration covered her upper lip.

'Any place she likes to go to get away, to relax?' Time to get to work.

'No. Ever since we've been – since I've known Wanda, she's never wanted to go away, never taken a vacation.'

'Sounds like a hard-working partner.'

'She is, very.'

'And what kind of lover?'

Beverly looked at me, staring hard into my eyes.

'Good,' she said firmly, her eyes darting from mine to her drink. 'Most of the time.' She took a long drink then looked back at me. There was some fresh pain in those blue eyes.

'If you've finished your drink, we should look inside for clues,' she commanded politely.

I winced at the word 'clues'. Since I rarely recognized a clue as such until it smacked me in the face, I hated being watched while I searched for the little buggers. Couldn't get out of it this time, though.

I followed Beverly back inside and through the house. Her familiarity told me it had been their home, hers and Wanda's. The furnishings were California contemporary – lots of casual fabrics, restful colors, natural woods, hints of the sea, suggestions of the desert. They seemed like Beverly's ideas. The Wanda touches were film scripts stacked and strewn around the living room with copies of the *Hollywood Reporter* thrown in for color.

'Wanda's the reader,' Beverly explained. 'I'm the people-watcher.'

And the one to watch, I thought, admiringly.

The kitchen had an abandoned look. As I opened cupboards, one after another, to find emptiness, Beverly confirmed my suspicion.

'Cooking never held much fascination for Wanda, so I took all the kitchen equipment when I left.'

12

'Did she ever ask what this room was for?'

Beverly smiled and I sighed. Lovely, that smile.

The bedroom looked comfortable and thoroughly understood. It contained, barely, a brass bed, high and wide and gleaming. Four over-sized pillows stood up against the headboard, each one with a different colored case. The bed coverings were neatly in place and a pair of dark blue cotton pajamas lay folded at the end of the bed.

I noticed something missing from one wall.

'What was here?' I asked, pointing out the dingy wall surrounding a clean patch.

Beverly looked stunned and took a moment to answer.

'My portrait,' she said quietly. 'I guess she didn't want to look at me anymore.'

'Is anything else missing? Look around,' I prompted.

Beverly went through the closet while I surveyed the top of the nightstand next to the bed. It held the standard fare – a lamp, a clock radio, and some paperbacks. Detective novels, three of them, with stiff covers and broken spines. Recently purchased, recently read.

'Her overnight bag is gone, but I can't be sure about the clothes,' Beverly reported.

We went through the house once more, looking for anything unusual. The clues weren't jumping up to introduce themselves. The bathroom appeared freshly cleaned, but the smell of Lysol didn't inspire any startling realizations. The few plants around were healthy, though suffering from the heat. The same could be said for Beverly and me. We met again in the bedroom.

'You mentioned on the phone that she missed a meeting. Where and what time?' I asked as Beverly sat down on the bed.

'Two o'clock at Tommy Tang's.'

I had passed the trendy West Hollywood eatery on my way there.

'When was the appointment set up?' I leaned against the wall where the portrait had been.

'Yesterday.'

13

'Who were you meeting?'

'An agent who has been all over us to cast "the next James Dean".'

'Isn't it difficult to work with an ex?'

'Sometimes. But we could hardly avoid each other in such a small community, now could we?'

I had to agree with her. The social avenues used by most lesbians virtually guaranteed run-ins to former lovers, even in LA.

'So, you get along? Still friends?' I pressed.

'Yes, still good friends.'

'Why did you break up?'

Beverly trained ice-cold blue eyes on me again.

'I don't see that that is any of your business,' she said.

If 'why' was a button, 'when' probably was, too. I backed off the personal stuff.

'Maybe she had another appointment.'

'No, I checked with Ronald, her secretary. Her schedule was clear,' she said calmly.

'Have you asked the police to find Wanda?'

'I called them. They won't accept a missing person report for twenty-four hours. They weren't convinced that something has happened to her.'

'What makes you think something has?'

Beverly slumped back against the brass headboard and covered her face with her hands.

'She told you about the phone calls, the car that tried to run her off the road. She's been seeing someone she shouldn't be seeing. Maybe a married woman. Men are not very understanding about their wives sleeping with other women, as I'm sure you know.' She looked up and smiled wanly.

'Not first-hand.' I didn't smile back. 'What's this woman's name?'

'I don't know. I really don't know anything except that Wanda has been uptight for weeks now.' She sat up straight.

'Is this woman the reason you split up?' I sat down on the bed next to her.

She looked away and blinked quickly several times.

14

'I couldn't believe it when I found out.' She faced me, clear-eyed. 'After all we had been to each other – friends, lovers, partners. Her arrogance was unbelievable!'

'So why are you so concerned about her now?'

'She's still my friend, despite all that has happened. And she is my business partner, after all. I must do the right thing by her, don't you agree?' She knitted her brow in a serious manner.

'Sure. But I'll need more to go on than just a maybe married woman and her cuckolded husband.'

'Just tell me what you want.'

She was in my arms before I could say 'Mary Astor'. Her hot slender fingers caressed the back of my neck. I felt flushed, the blood pounding in my head, as Beverly pulled me toward her. That kiss sealed my fate.

I left Wanda's house an hour later with a list of her friends, a check for two hundred dollars, and a little confusion over whether I had taken advantage of Beverly or she had taken advantage of me. It didn't really matter; we both had enjoyed ourselves, heat and all.

At the end of the street, I pulled into a driveway and waited for Beverly to go past. The white Mercedes zipped by about five minutes later. With the coast clear, I returned to Wanda's.

Parking in the carport, I noticed a large rug covering something square at the rear of the structure. When I lifted the rug, I was face-to-face with a life-sized image of Beverly Grayson, wearing nothing but a Panama hat. I stepped back to take in the full effect of the painting. Beverly sat cross-legged on a large lush pillow decorated with a tropical print. Her hair, past waist-length, was strategically arranged so that it barely covered her breasts, tantalizing the beholder of the scene. Her smile of slight amusement was designed to launch magnificent rumors about its source. I put the rug back over the frame canvas. The effect of the painting was almost as overwhelming as Beverly herself. I understood why Wanda had taken it down.

Back on the job, I jimmied the lock on the side door, just like Uncle Raymond had taught me, and went inside. I went back to the bedroom to check out the closet for myself this time. The clothes rack didn't give up anything, but the shoe rack on the floor did. Three pairs of prongs were empty.

A personal phone directory next to the telephone in the living room had caught my eye earlier. When I opened it, a list of speed-dial codes and numbers sat on the top. Naturally, I filched the list. Beverly had given me the names of three people – Kellie Banks, Betty Smith, and Ronald Thomas, Wanda's secretary. Who had only three friends? Wanda's speed-dial list had Ronald's number on the top line followed by a dozen others. The name Emily MacNeil and a local phone number was penciled in at the very top of the page. Betty Smith wasn't on the list. I dialed the number Beverly had written down next to the name. The man who answered said no one named Smith lived there.

Kellie Banks, the name under Ronald's on Wanda's list, had a West Hollywood exchange, indicating that she probably lived just to the south, so I gave her a call next.

According to Ms Banks, she hadn't seen Wanda James for at least three weeks and she didn't care if she never saw her again. Seems that Wanda had made a pass at Kellie's girlfriend at a Memorial Day barbecue. If Wanda had disappeared, Kellie thought it likely that she'd run off with somebody else's partner.

I learned that much on the phone. When I asked to stop by, Kellie agreed immediately. Wanda and Beverly, apparently, was an irresistible subject for discussion.

A short time later I stood on the front porch of Kellie's small duplex. Once inside, I took an iced tea and another scathing earful about Wanda from the middle-aged woman. Kellie's paintings covered her living room walls, while an easel was propped open in the dining room, which also served as an art studio.

'Does Wanda make a habit of chasing other women's lovers?' I asked once we sat down.

'Wanda makes a habit of chasing women,' Kellie answered

with a firm nod of her smallish head. A dollop of gray paint clumped a few strands of her black hair together just above her right eyebrow.

'So, she and Beverly had an open relationship?' I ventured.

'Beverly sent you here, right?' I nodded. 'You don't know her, though, do you?' I shook my head, no. 'Beverly is loyal to a fault. And Wanda is that fault. She forgave Wanda time and again, believing her when she said she'd never do it again. Until this last time.'

'You mean the married woman?' I asked.

'I don't know if she was married or not. But, whoever it was, it was the last straw for Beverly. She moved out and told Wanda their relationship was strictly business from now on.'

'How long ago was that?'

'A couple of months or so.'

'What do you think made Beverly change?'

'I heard that Wanda brazenly brought her paramour-of-the-month to an office party. Beverly was mortified.'

'But you don't have any idea who that was?'

'Who could keep up with Wanda's women?' Kellie laughed.

I thanked her for the cold drink and her time.

As Kellie walked me to the door, I asked how she had come to know Wanda and Beverly.

'Beverly commissioned me to paint her portrait about a year ago. It was a birthday present. Wanda loved it, just loved it. But all the while Beverly was sitting for me, I had the distinct impression she was really having the portrait done for herself. I was surprised to hear she didn't take it with her when she moved out.'

'Wanda has taken it down now,' I told Kellie.

'Probably too hard to look at what she can't have anymore.'

I took my leave and thanked my lucky stars once again that people love to talk about their friends.

Since I was near home, I stopped off to shower and change clothes. As I unlocked the door, the stale, hot, smog-tinged air hit me like exhaust from a bus on a tour of the stars' homes. The first order of business, I decided, was to turn on the box fan. I dropped the mail on the kitchen table and checked with my answering service. Jane gave me two messages – one from my last client, insisting that the check was in the mail, and one from Gayle, my mechanic, saying the Riley was running like clockwork once again. Jane wished me a cool night and gave me the impression she would have accepted an offer for a hot one. But the humidity was too high, and I had work to do.

I showered and found another set of whites for the evening. A black, loosely-knotted tie added some contrast and a summer-weight fedora, also black, added some class.

With picking up the Riley, rustling up some dinner, and trying to find Wanda James all vying to be next on the agenda, I called Ronald Thomas, Wanda's secretary. Sure, he said, I could come over, providing I made it quick. Sounded like a busy chap.

Before leaving, I tried calling the penciled-in name on Wanda's phone list, Emily MacNeil, but there was no answer. Another time, Emily.

The short drive to Santa Monica Boulevard and the garage was pleasant enough in eighty-five degrees. Friday night brought out all the neighborhood variety. Two grandmothers, round and soft, sat on the sidewalk in kitchen chairs, swapping complaints about the snores of old men. Dark-haired olive-skinned boys pedaled black bicycles in and out of the street. Their little sisters squealed through a game of tag. As I got closer to the Boulevard, the children gave way to adolescents, fashion victims and rock 'n roll casualties, and no-deposit, no-return runaways. Home sweet home. The boys, the girls, the men about to cruise, the women about to work – the street had room for them all. And me, too.

The Riley kicked over perfectly. I put the top down. It's going to be a fine night, I thought, as I slid behind the wheel and waved a quick goodbye to Gayle. It's always a fine night when I'm working and the Riley's working at the same time.

Ronald lived in Silver Lake, so I took Santa Monica to Sunset Boulevard and the heart of the district. Along the way, the royal blue Riley attracted its usual number of admiring looks and 'what is it?' questions. It had been Uncle Raymond's pride and joy, and I knew why every time I drove the British sportster. The large fenders, the remnant of a running board, the front grillwork, the leather seats, all gave me a rush of the 'forties. Boplicity!


'You must be Wiggins, right?' Ronald answered the door.

'Yes.' I extended my hand, which he took for a second.

'Come in, come in.' He stepped back and waved me in. 'I have to finish dressing, but we can talk. Sit, sit.'

I sat down as Ronald, tall, thin, and slightly balding, padded away in bare feet. He returned a minute later with some socks and western boots. He sat across from me on a leather couch.

'So, on the phone you said something about Wanda?' He started putting on the socks.

'Right. She's apparently missing, and Beverly has hired me to find her.'

'No, she's not.'

'She's not what?'

'Missing.'

'How do you know?'

'Because she told me she was going to her beach house this weekend.'

'And you didn't tell Beverly?'

'Wanda told me not to. She said Beverly would be better off if she didn't know about her plans.'

'Did those plans involve a married woman?'

'Not *very* married, if she can get away for the weekend, wouldn't you say?'

'Beverly mentioned Wanda had an appointment with an agent. Know anything about it?'

'Sure. Beverly told me to remind Wanda about it, so I called Wanda in Malibu this morning.' Ronald left the room again.

'This morning?' I called after him. There was no answer

until he returned, putting a leather vest on over his white western shirt.

'What?'

'You talked to Wanda *this* morning?'

'Actually I talked to Emily. She said Wanda was cooling off or something.' He looked at himself approvingly in a full-length mirror on the back of the front door.

'What did she mean?'

'They had just had an argument, you know, a lover's quarrel.'

'Is Emily's last name MacNeil?'

'Yep.' Ronald took a pair of spurs off the hat rack on the wall and sat down again.

'And Beverly didn't know anything about Wanda's being at her beach house?'

'Nope. It was just our little secret. Are you going to tell her?' He put the spurs on the boots.

'She hired me to find Wanda. Wanda didn't hire me not to.'

'If you tell her, it's my ass, I'm sure.' Ronald stood up and walked around the room, listening to the spurs jingle-jangle. 'Beverly'll probably get hysterical again.'

'You don't see too many people wearing spurs in LA anymore,' I said as I stood up.

'You just don't go to the right places, Wiggins.'

'Don't they get a little dangerous on the dance floor?'

'Only if you move your feet.' He winked.

The doorbell rang and Ronald's date arrived. I had one more question for Ronald.

'Why would Beverly get hysterical about Wanda's weekend plans?'

'Because, up until about three weeks ago, Beverly and Emily were The Hot Twosome around town.'

I wished the cowboys happy trails and headed for the nearest payphone.

One number on Wanda's list had the word 'beach' next to it. I dropped in my twenty cents and marveled at my knack for finding missing people. A busy signal rewarded my

20

cleverness. I waited a few minutes and tried the number again. Still busy. I tried another number.

Beverly answered immediately after the first ring.

'I think I've located Wanda.'

'So soon?'

'You're paying me to be efficient. I need your help to make sure she's okay.'

'I'm also paying you to be effective, darling. What kind of help could you possibly need from me?'

'I think Wanda's at her beach house.'

'So you're going to Malibu?'

'Why not drive out there together? You know where it is, right?'

'You go, sweetheart. This afternoon has left me exhausted.'

Her tone puzzled and stroked me at the same time. I gambled for some clarity.

'She may be with Emily MacNeil.' I tossed out the name for effect.

'So she's seeing that precious little bird again,' Beverly said archly. 'I'm not surprised. Well, tell Wanda she'd better have another excuse for missing the meeting today.'

Obviously, the boss had no intention of going to Malibu with me, so I wrote down the directions to the beach house and said I'd call her from there.

'Thanks so much, darling. I don't know what I would have done without you,' Beverly purred across the telephone line.

I found myself saying, 'Don't worry, honey, I'll take care of everything,' and wondering what the hell I meant.

I went to Canter's for some dinner and some time. Loretta, the waitress, gave me both with a smile and no chitchat.

Beverly had seemed so concerned about Wanda this afternoon. On the phone, though, she sounded indifferent to news of Wanda. The more I thought about her story, the more holes I saw. A warning bell was sounding. Beautiful women are a dangerous weakness in any line of work. And most of the time I didn't even try to resist their charms. Beverly had plenty not to resist. But just how many times had I been seduced so far on this case? Where was Wanda

21

James? Did it matter? And Emily MacNeil was beginning to sound like the stuff dreams are made of. Or nightmares.

The beach house was located in the far north end of Malibu, where the rich not only had the sand and the surf, but the space to enjoy them. My puzzlement over Beverly was pushed aside as I got closer and closer to the house. By the time I pulled into the driveway of Wanda's hideaway and got out of the Riley, I had my old spring back. My heart had back its old song. Life was good, it was cool.

I knocked on the door. The door opened slightly from the pressure of my knock. I pushed it back slowly. The pulsating sound of a telephone left off the hook too long came from somewhere inside.

Moonlight flooded the dark room, revealing the standard living room arrangement of couch framed by chairs and end tables. I saw something long and lumpy on the couch. Five cautious steps and I was staring at a nude woman I had never seen before. Laid out, she was, waiting for a dirge to begin.

Blue ocean, cool breezes, moonlight shimmering, Beverly dancing slowly, closer, closer. The moonlight makes an aura around her, silky white, swaying closer, closer. Hair flying gently and hands touching softly, cool skin on cool skin. Warm lips brush, tingling, the blue starts to turn green, moonlight bleaches to sunlight. Closer, closer, Beverly caressing, covering. Flesh on flesh, steaming in the too-bright whiteness. Circles, pools of sweat engulf the tropical bed. Drenching, drained, soaking wet, stone dead.

I came to. Lying next to a couch on a scratchy carpet with an even worse headache than I had brought from LA, I had the overwhelming desire to be someplace else. Anyplace else.

A lamp on a table at the far end of the couch had been turned on since my entrance. I sat up slowly, leaning upright against the chair nearest the door. The woman I had seen just before hitting the floor was still lying on the couch. A blanket had been spread over her body since my last glimpse.

Rubbing the place where the throbbing was the worst, I discovered a tender bump at the base of my skull. The room was still and much too quiet.

I stood up to take a closer look at the body. The room started spinning. I sat down and contemplated my silent companion. She looked to be in her late twenties, a little on the frail side. There was blood on the side of her mouth and bruises on her neck. Her face had a repose to it that suggested peaceful slumber. Once the nauseous feeling subsided, I reached over toward her wrist and checked for a pulse. The coldness of the flesh told me it was a waste of time. She had been dead for a spell, maybe hours.

A tiny stream of sweat ran down my back. Murder was not what I was looking for. A little romance, a little excitement, maybe a car chase here and there, but not the big M. 'Alibi' suddenly had new meaning in my life.

'Forget something? Or do you just want to make sure you've done the job right?' Wanda's voice boomed at me from behind.

I whirled to face her and found a gun directed at the general vicinity of my heart.

'I came looking for you,' I told her, fighting back the nausea that threatened to overtake me.

'That's a likely story. Why? Am I missing or something?'

Her jaw was set firmly and her lips pursed intently. Big-boned and muscular, her body was taut, yet tentative as she stood in the middle of the room. A well-timed 'boo' would have sent her ten feet in the air. The dampness of her Hawaiian shirt suggested that Wanda had been sweating it out a while.

'Beverly thought you were. She hired me to find you.'

'Oh, I'm sure she put you up to all of this. How long have you two been planning this?'

'Planning what?' I asked innocently.

'You're good at playing dumb, Wiggins. *If* you're playing.'

I winced. Sticks and stones . . .

'Wanda, I really don't know what you're talking about.'

'Which one of you actually killed Emily?'

23

Wanda's unsteady pistol hand betrayed the serious cold-ness in her eyes. I tried to think of a way to put some distance between myself and this obviously distraught woman. But I was faced with an uncharacteristic lack of inspiration.

'Listen, Wanda, that nighty-night rap you gave me has made it hard to be as sharp as I would like during a conver-sation where my life hangs in the balance. Do you think I could have some ice and a towel?'

'Help yourself. The kitchen's that way.'

Wanda motioned toward the far end of the living room. She followed me closely as I headed toward the slight relief of a cold compress.

I leaned against the sink as Wanda stood in the doorway, blocking the only obvious escape route. As if I were capable of moving that fast.

'So, how much are you getting for this?' Wanda jerked her head toward the living room.

'You're not in a position to be pinning raps,' I said. 'After all, it's your house, your girlfriend, your ex-girlfriend's ex. And you and Emily had a fight just this morning, didn't you? Could be jealous rage reared its ugly head.'

'You're a real smart-ass aren't you, Wiggins?' Wanda began to seethe. 'Oh, yes, jealous rage is right. You and Beverly are perfect for each other. Two of the high and mighty ones. You both think you can get by on your good looks and everybody else's hard work. Beverly used me and she's using you. She even tried to use Emily.' Wanda's voice trailed off as she let out a long cracked breath. 'Emily and I argued over when I should leave the agency. She thought I should give Beverly more notice.'

I wiped my face with the compress and got a whiff of familiar perfume. I took another hit. Having a keen sense of smell always had been a blessing, but never handier than on this job. The perfume was unmistakably Beverly's.

The picture was getting fuzzier and it had nothing to do with my concussion. My gut said Wanda didn't kill Emily. My ego wouldn't let me believe that Beverly had and then set me up to take the fall.

'Did you have a business appointment scheduled today?'
I asked.

'Yeah, Beverly arranged it.' Tears stained Wanda's cheeks.

'Where?'

'Newport Beach. I was two hours down there and two hours back on the damned freeway for nothing.'

'What do you mean?'

'The guy with "the next James Dean" never showed.'

'When did you get back here?'

'Right before you came in. I hadn't even put on the lights.'

It took some smooth talking, but I convinced Wanda that we needed Beverly to find out what happened to Emily, and Beverly wasn't about to come to Malibu. I suggested Wanda call the police and bring them to my office in an hour. She listened as I phoned Beverly and told her to meet me there, too. Beverly balked at first. But when I mentioned I might need an alibi, she found a reason to be there. I left Wanda sitting quietly beside Emily's body.

The trip back saw my headache increase ever so much and my confusion diminish ever so slightly. I turned off the Pacific Coast Highway at Sunset and headed for West Hollywood, anxious to put some questions to Beverly before the coppers arrived.

The streets of the city were far from deserted that time of the night, but the deep shadows made the desperate side of the urban life more evident. I startled a prostitute and her customer negotiating in the doorway of the Somner Building when I walked up. We all apologized for being there.

Up on the fourth floor, I unlocked the outer office door with no sign of Beverly. My shorts stuck to me like used gum. The building was a swelter box at night, without air conditioning. Flipping on the lights to both offices, I crossed to the inner office and began opening windows.

As I reached the last window, Beverly walked in, dressed in an aquamarine jumpsuit that did everything for her eyes. The still-fresh image of young Emily MacNeil kept me from being more than momentarily distracted.

25

'You sounded so serious on the phone, darling. Is anything wrong?' Beverly asked as she entered the office.

'I'm afraid so. I have some bad news for you sweetheart,' I said.

'You know, I'm very glad to see you,' Beverly moved closer to me.

You may not be in a few minutes, I thought, stepping away from her and toward the liquor cabinet.

'Can I get you a drink?' I asked.

'I'll take Scotch, if you have it, with a little water,' she said, smiling.

I fixed Beverly's drink and a gin and tonic for myself, while Beverly sat stiffly on the worn couch. I felt the gulf between us grow. The stone-coldness behind the smoldering blue eyes was glinting through.

'I didn't find Wanda,' I told her as I handed her the drink.

'You said she was at the beach house.'

'I said I *thought* she was at the beach house. I did find a woman there. But she couldn't tell me anything about Wanda.'

Beverly took a drink before she asked, 'Why not?'

'Because she was dead.'

'How awful! What happened?'

'It looks like murder.'

'Do you think Wanda killed her?'

'It's possible. It may explain why Wanda disappeared. Anyway, I thought you might want to call a lawyer before I call the police.'

'Me? Why should I call a lawyer?'

'For Wanda.'

'Oh, of course.'

'In the meantime, I'll keep looking for her,' I said as I finished my drink. 'And her current flame.'

'I thought you said you found Emily at the Beach house.'

'I found a murdered young woman. I don't know who she was.'

I took a long drink as Beverly tried to avoid reacting to her slip.

26

'Tell me about your break-up with Wanda,' I said.

'It was over Emily, of course,' she asserted coolly. 'Wanda was cheating on me and I wouldn't stand for it.'

'It wasn't the first time Wanda had cheated on you.'

She took in the statement with no visible reaction.

'I mean, Wanda sort of made a habit of cheating, didn't she?' I pressed.

'She's easily flattered. We run into a lot of young actresses, eager to get into the movies, and, well, Wanda allows their flirtations to go to her head.'

'But what made Emily MacNeil different? Why split up over one more pretty face?'

'Wanda was making a fool of me in public,' Beverly said matter-of-factly. 'Emily was making a fool of Wanda, encouraging her to give up the agency and become a screenwriter, of all things!'

'Did you hire me to take the rap for you or for Wanda?'

A knock on the door froze Beverly's look of surprise.

'That'll be Wanda,' I said as I left the room.

By the time I let Wanda in and we returned to the inner office, Beverly had recovered her familiar poise and was standing behind my desk. Wanda and I stopped dead in our tracks at the sight of my gun in Beverly's steady hand.

'Move over there.' Beverly motioned toward the couch with the pistol. 'Both of you.'

Wanda edged out of her line of fire.

'That gun's not loaded, Beverly,' I said. 'I just keep it around to show clients who think detectives should pack hardware.'

Beverly looked at me then looked at the gun. She aimed at Wanda's chest and pulled the trigger. Twice. She pointed the .38 at me for the third try. How did I get so lucky as to be with not one, but two women who would have killed me? I took the useless weapon from Beverly as she staggered wearily to the couch.

'The police are on the way,' Wanda said as I put the gun back in the top desk drawer.

Beverly stood up and made a dash for the door. Catching

27

her arm, Wanda slammed the door and locked it before she could escape.

'You're not going anywhere!' Wanda spat at her as she shoved Beverly in my direction.

I caught her before she could fall against the desk. When I looked into her stone-cold blue eyes, the Beverly I had felt close to a few hours before wasn't there.

'Let me go,' she pleaded. 'I'll give you five thousand dollars.'

I raised my eyebrows.

'Ten thousand,' she offered.

'How about the truth?' I counter-offered.

'The truth?' She wheeled out of my grasp to face the door Wanda stood blocking. 'You mean the truth about Wanda's ingratitude and disloyalty?

'Who gave you your start, Wanda?' Beverly hissed. 'Who taught you how to land the big contracts? Who made sure you could afford that Ferrari? How many times did I take you back, Wanda? And what have you done for me? You cheated, you lied, and then you let this parasite Emily make a shambles of the best agency in the business!'

'She was good for me, Beverly. I know you tried to seduce her, tried to poison her against me. But you and I were through and nothing was going to change that.'

'Who are you to decide we were through? No one leaves me! I leave them!' Beverly screamed at Wanda.

'You left Emily dead!' Wanda screamed back.

'Liar!' Beverly ignored Wanda and turned toward me. 'Don't you see I could never kill anyone? You found Emily dead in Wanda's house. Wanda obviously has a vile temper and no scruples. Let's turn her over to the police and get out of here. We can go anywhere you want.' The smoldering look came back into her eyes. I was getting pretty heated myself.

'But angel, what makes you think you can get away with it?' I asked.

The perspiration beaded on her upper lip.

'With your help, the police will believe me. I called you

28

because I was concerned for my missing friend, remember? And everyone knows I liked Emily enormously. Why would I harm her?'

'Why, indeed? Could it be you'd met your match? Not only was Emily taking your woman, but threatening your livelihood and resisting your charms as well. So, you sent Wanda on a wild goose chase to Newport Beach, strangled the young lady, and called me for a cover. Not a bad day's work.'

'You're too smart for your own good, Wiggins.'

'No,' Wanda said. 'Too smart for *your* own good.'

Another knock on the outer door told us that the Los Angeles country sheriff's deputies had arrived. Beverly took my arm as Wanda went to let them in.

'Please, you don't want to do this. You can't do this to me. Whatever you want, just tell me. We're a good team. I thought you wanted me. . . .'

Her smoldering eyes were there, but all I could think about was the cold clammy wrist of Emily MacNeil.

'I depended on you, just like I depended on Wanda. All I get is betrayal. It's just not fair,' Beverly lamented as a female deputy escorted her from the office.

Wanda and I followed the squad car to the sheriff's station to give our statements.

I left the station just as dawn broke. Beverly had had it all – looks, money, success. But looks, money and success aren't everything, as my granny used to say. You gotta have all your marbles to stay in the game.

The California Savings and Loan sign flashed seventy-five degrees and 6:05 a.m. when I drove by. Another scorcher on its way. I checked into the Best Western on Fairfax and turned the air conditioning up to high before hitting the sack. Twelve hours later I checked out, much cooler.

The final act of the case played a few months later. Wanda called one day to say she was leaving LA. I stopped by that evening to wish her well.

The U-Haul truck was all packed and the canyon house

was bare. Beverly's portrait leaned against a wall in the empty living room.

'Where are you going?' I asked.

'San Francisco. I hear the women are real friendly there.'

'You can never have too much of a good thing.'

'Are you taking the painting?'

'No. I thought you might want it. You had a real case for her, didn't you?'

So, Beverly, wearing just a Panama hat and very long hair, hangs on my office wall now. And Wanda James visits her ex-lover every couple of months at the California Institute for Women in Fontana.

# THE BARBER HAS KILLED HIS WIFE

## Albert Cossery

*Albert Cossery (1913– ) was born and educated in Egypt. In 1945 he moved to Paris where he has lived ever since. His novels include* La Maison de la Mort Certaine *and* Une Ambition Dans Le Desert.

*'The Barber Has Killed His Wife' is set in Cairo and is from a collection entitled* Les Hommes Oublié de Dieu. *It was originally published in English in 1945. As the story's translator ('H.E.') wrote at that time, here: 'We are at rock-bottom; a submarine world where poverty looms gigantic and real. And we see its consequences in terms of human suffering –.'*

It was in Black Lane.

This evening Chaktour the tinker, who was at work in his shop on the repair of a toilet jug, left his job for an instant to collect himself and to think calmly about his miserable and infinite life. But he did not pursue these bitter reflections very far. His whole life was there, close to him, and he could touch it with his hands, so drab and dirty it was, without a shred of vision. He was so frankly disgusted by it that he thought of something else.

In the first place he tried to understand how it was that Saadi the barber had poisoned his wife. (At this period it was the supreme preoccupation of the lane's intellects.) But the details of this shadowy crime were lacking to him and he had to resign himself to giving it up. Anyhow, the business was so fishy that it was better not to touch it, even in thought. Didn't they say that the police had arrested certain clients of the unfortunate Saadi, to interrogate them and

31

establish their moral responsibility according to the degree of relationship they had with the barber? Even the words of one of them, Haroussi the people's restaurant-keeper, were judged full of provocation. This ignoble *restaurateur* had said one day, it appeared, to the itinerant barber: 'Saadi my son, the man who can get rid of his wife will surely go to Paradise.' Without doubt, these words of deep wisdom had been ill interpreted by the barber. At all events no Paradise wanted him for the moment and the police thus found themselves compelled to keep him in prison, just like a vulgar assassin. 'Poor Saadi, you used to shave my beard so well for the bit of bread that I gave you. What's going to happen to us if all the men like you go to prison?' Chaktour had never been in prison. Then he thought about the prison regime, about the suffering endured by the prisoners, above all their fleshy solitude. But on this again he had no precise ideas. He stopped in his imaginary deductions and looked into the lane.

Opposite the shop was street lamp No. 329, which squandered its official brightness over the entire lane. Sometimes a passer-by with vague face stopped in the zone of light to examine himself before returning home, or, for the tenth time at least, to look at a false coin which Saroukh the café proprietor had just given him. Some dogs also roamed in the lane, starving skeletons, protected by mange. There was always a woman cursing her children in a high and strident voice, for the whole lane to hear, so that persons of bad faith should know that she was occupied with the education of her own. And everywhere, more or less, without preference, garbage was scattered.

Bad luck to the poor man with leisure. Chaktour was about to set to work again when he saw the child. He stood at the entrance to the shop, carrying under his arm the pile of clover which he had just bought in the market. And he looked at his father with an air of reproach in his sad eyes, as if to remind him of something serious which the man had forgotten.

'What are you bringing me that for, little one?'

32

'It's for the sheep, father.'

'What sheep?'

Why didn't he understand? The child was on the point of crying, but he forced back his tears and explained everything to this father dulled by misery, the slave of a rigorous and cruel fate.

'The holiday sheep, father. I've looked after the clover. Now it only remains for you to buy the sheep.'

The child was dirty but handsome. He was naked under his earth-coloured robe. He bore his sadness in all his body.

Chaktour looked at his son with amazement and pity. He said nothing. In his ceaselessly-tortured spirit there was no more room for a new grief. Simply, he felt crushed by his son's deed; for he understood now that in this child – his flesh and his blood – there was forming a real and conscious misery which he had not noticed up to now and which from henceforth would remain bound to his own. For how long? The child would grow and with him would grow his misery, until the day when, weary in his turn – for can a man support his misery alone? – he would create a son to share the burden with him. The poor man's sole consolation is that he does not leave, when he dies, a prodigal son. The ignominy which he hands on to his descendants is inexhaustible.

'The holiday is not for us, my son,' he said. 'We are poor.'

The child cried, cried bitterly.

'What's that to me? I want a sheep.'

'We are poor,' repeated Chaktour.

'And why are we poor?' asked the child.

The man reflected before answering. He himself, after so many years of tenacious indigence, did not know why they were poor. It came from far back, from so far that Chaktour could not recall how it had begun. He told himself that, no doubt, his misery had never had a beginning. It was a misery which extended beyond men, and without troubling itself about the will of men. It had taken hold of him from birth, and he had belonged to it at once, without the least resistance, for he had been bound to it long before he was born, while still in his mother's womb.

33

The child was still waiting to be told why they were poor. He had stopped crying, but there were still many tears inside him, all the tears of miserable children whose dreams are betrayed by life.

'Listen, little one: go and sit down in the corner and let me work. If we are poor it is because God has forgotten us, my son.'

'God!' said the child. 'And when will he remember us, father?'

'When God forgets someone, my son, it is for ever.'

'All the same, I'll keep the clover,' said the child.

He carried off his pile of clover, put it in a corner of the shop, then squatted down on it. And he began to cry again, because he was little and it was his own fashion of revolting against the injustice of the world. Sharply the child learnt that he was alone in life, sharply he entered into contact with the unknown world of distress, of pitiful human distress.

The man, for his part, set to work once more. The sight of that little face ravaged by tears gave him a sick feeling. He suffered in a new and terrible fashion. But what did it matter, his pain and the pain of all the men in the universe? The important thing was that the child could not suffer any longer. More and more he recognised this essential truth. The child! who would attend to saving the child? As he worked the man thought of death as the only possible deliverance, and he desired it ardently for himself, his wife, his child and all the lane.

At this moment up came Gohloche the policeman, haughty and arrogant as ever.

He stopped before the shop and let his execrable gaze wander over the man and his son. Gohloche the policeman was a born torturer. In his look there was a stupidity which struck you dead. And he stayed there, upright, muffled in his heavy cape of black wool, like a noxious and powerful animal. It was cold. The child stopped crying; he was frightened. This policeman who had just risen like another might in the night, terrified him. He felt suffocated. He thought of his mother. He longed for a little warmth. He closed his eyes,

34

thinking thus to escape the sombre destiny which menaced him outside. The pile of clover, beneath him, flattened out slowly. For an instant he had a vision of a beautiful fat sheep which belonged to no one, a sheep free as the dogs and cats which circulated in the lane.

Chaktour preserved an enigmatic silence. He seemed to be ignorant of the policeman's presence. He was still tormenting himself about the itinerant barber. 'Why did Saadi poison his wife?' this question preoccupied him gravely, as if it were at the root of all his misfortunes. The itinerant barber's crime had taught him how far the hand of man would go. It was unheard of, what a man could perpetrate. 'Here is a man who poisons his wife. Why? Saadi himself, he ought to know. One day I shall go and pay him a visit in prison; he will tell me.' Now he thought no more of anything. In his corner the child, crouching over his pile of clover, seemed to be dead. A rat slid along the wall. The policeman wanted to speak, but he felt a sudden fit of weakness, as if he had just smelt a nauseating stench. It was because of this sadness which reigned in the shop and was not within the measurement of man. Street lamp No. 329 was still squandering its light without regard to expense.

Gohloche the policeman quickly recovered; he was not a sentimental man. He set his weakness down to fatigue. The evening before he had given battle to a squad of streetsweepers who were simply demanding not to die of hunger. His intervention in this affair had been adjudged in high quarters as meriting every praise. Had he not, alone, laid out with his truncheon a respectable number of these bastards of sweepers? Nothing better could have happened to him. He was on the high-road to promotion. Then why did the sight of this shop oppress him to such an extent? He didn't understand. So he became unpleasant. His gaze searched everywhere with insistence, and succeeded in detecting the pile of clover. He gave a smile which was like the reflection of an anonymous god.

'So, Chaktour my father, you have bought the clover to attract the sheep? Do you think that a sheep lets itself be

35

caught like a rat? Upon my honour you are becoming spoiled, O man!'

The sound of his voice troubled the serenity of the black-beetles which were roaming tranquilly about the shop; they made for their holes at top speed. Gaping pots of tin gleamed in the shadows. The shop was only lit by the street lamp which stood opposite. The policeman, halted in front of the door, repelled this solitary brightness, which dashed itself to fragments on his back. Chaktour kept silent still: he had no wish to enter into conversation with this frightful policeman whose unpleasantness he knew so well. The only thing was that this forced obscurity prevented him from working. He would have liked to mend this toilet jug as quickly as possible and be able to go home. It was very cold too in this shop, above all for the child, who was naked under his robe. All this seemed to Chaktour of an unsurmountable horror. He had no more courage for anything; this evening he felt cru-shed by the weight of his whole life. This business of the clover and the sheep was the limit of what he could stand. The man was thinking, above all, of the child. For him a holiday had no meaning. 'We talk of a holiday, but really there is no holiday. Why did Saadi poison his wife? That is what people ought to be thinking about. There will be no holiday as long as we don't know why Saadi poisoned his wife.' He was haunted anew by the itinerant barber's crime. At the very end of his misery the man tried to understand. And it was good so.

'Son of a pig,' said the policeman, 'so you won't deign to answer me?'

The tinker realised the necessity of showing himself concili-atory to this cursed spectre of authority. He had enough trouble as it was. For a moment he fixed the policeman with a piteous air, and then said in correct and respectful language:

'We are your servants, O policeman Gohloche. Permit me to tell you that your august presence has made precious this humble shop.'

This compliment, uttered in a lamenting voice, immobilised the atmosphere like a lugubrious fantasy. The three personages of this scene were at that point of life where one no longer believes anything.

Gohloche the policeman personified the most hateful kind of wickedness, wickedness which is put to the service of the great ones of the earth. A buyable wickedness. It no longer belonged to him. He had sold it to the most competent people, who used it to subjugate and mortify an entire wretched nation. He was no longer master of his wickedness. He had to lead and direct it according to certain rules whose atrocity never varied.

Gohloche the policeman lived in Black Lane, but he exercised his function as tyrant in the centre of the European city. And for him it was a kind of death; he grew anæmic on it. For in such a district, frequented generally by Europeans, his ill-nature encountered serious obstacles. It could not expand at leisure. So Gohloche deflected his hate on to all the slaves furnished by the native element; street porters, beggars, little collectors of fag-ends, lepers and the blind, and the whole tribe of wanderers who do not succeed in dying because it takes a lot of time to kill them. This vermin, come there to give the European city its cachet of the gaudy Orient, was numerous. A blessed nourishment for the eyes of tourists. But Gohloche the policeman was no tourist and he understood nothing of exoticism.

It was nearly midnight. The European city, despite its modern buildings in eight storeys (with lift and running water), its brightly-lit cafés and its prostitutes wearing the pavement by their comings and goings, seemed a prey to a drab, ineffective boredom, born of doubt and the mediocrity of its pleasures. One felt that the city wished to live, that it had everything for the purpose, but that a sort of internal, pitiless distress held it immobile with its unnatural lights, its stupid women and its criminal ease. It has the perfect apathy of a glutted monster. It devoured all. It spread with a constant rage. On all sides one saw it coming. It grew into the desert, it grew into the palmgroves, and the islands on the other side of the river. One could no longer stop it. It was a

37

blossoming of blocks of flats and of sumptuous villas. Strange harlot's body: it spread in all directions, always venal, always interested. And the countryside fled before it, rapid and monotonous. The city chased it without respite. Accursed countryside, which went off to vomit its distress at the edges of the poorer quarters. For there, where misery lies too thick, the city halted its triumphal march. It took only the good lands. All that made life sweet and comfortable belonged to it. Pure air, drinkable water, electric light, all belonged to it. It had only scorned a little debris. And in this debris wilted the life of a whole people.

Civilisation became especially terrible all along Fouad the First Street and Emad el Din Street. In fact, these two principal streets enjoyed all that a civilised town maintains and showers forth for the degradation of man. There were shows without taste, bars where alcohol was very dear, cabarets with easy girls, fashionable shops, jewellers and even luminous signs. Nothing was lacking to the banquet. One could degrade oneself *ad nauseam*.

Meanwhile the city swarmed with a multitude of creatures that had nothing to do with this disorder and these lights. They moved near all these lights like fearful shadows. They looked at all the fine things of the city with the eyes of brutes that do not understand. They carried with them their muddy quarter and their filthy misery. They were visible as wounds. One chased them away, but they insisted on staying. One reason, sufficient and implacable, drew them into this magic ring: hunger. It was a thing which they knew well. They were innumerable, around the restaurants, around all the places where one eats. For them, eating was everything. They desired nothing else. For generations they had had no other desires. They were ignoble and soulless bodies. It pained the city to hold them; it pained civilisation to see them. They looked like remorse; very ancient remorse rooted in the soil. But for all that they did not want to die. To beg a bit of bread from those who had taken all from them, was still, for them, a chance to live. And they were called beggars or thieves according to their insistence on living.

For the moment this was what was happening at the top of Fouad the First Street, exactly by a ladies' shoe shop. A team of street sweepers was resting at this spot, waiting for the arrival of the comrades they were supposed to relieve. They were huddled one against the other, not so much to warm themselves as to render themselves inoffensive as possible and not to disturb decent people by their presence. These street sweepers were the most wretched things in the world. Usually they were taciturn and reserved. But this evening one felt that they were living in an unaccustomed and tragic fashion. A singular animation was making them move and talk with authority. They really looked like men; but one saw that it was only a beginning. There was ample hope that they would become completely men. A will to revolt was showing itself in them like a new puberty. And this puberty was making them care, for the first time, about a better life. They did not know to what point this will might lead them. The road to be run was too long, and they shivered at the edge of it, for by living so long without moving, their limbs were soft and their eyes blinded with shadows.

There they were, heaped on the pavement like survivors of a country ravaged by famine. They wore uniforms which were new but not fit for the time of year. They were uniforms of light cloth which the administration responsible for clothing them had given them in mid-December. A number were barefooted. The cold went right through them, and they coughed in turn, each after his fashion. From time to time one of them would light a piece of paper which flared up and then went out immediately, after having produced a fugitive warmth. Then, around this slender gleam the faces of these men stood out with violence. They had the faces of a fearful humanity. Seeing them together like this in the middle of this clean and civilised street, one was tempted to shout for help. But the indifference which surrounded them, broke them completely. They were alone against the invincible power which made slaves of them. In snatching them from their role of human beings, this power had reduced

39

them to their proper limits. They did not expect the help of anyone; they heard no foreign voice. They heard only the still uncertain murmur of their revolt.

They seemed to be plotting against themselves, their councils were so full of precautions and of care. They advanced in their revolt with a thousand hesitations. They scratched their bodies with large gestures and spat their catarrh down beside them, gently, like a precious thing. The fine Fouad the First Street found itself, in this spot, with its reputation genuinely damaged. This mob of sweepers was not pleasing in its picturesqueness. It was rather sinister. The street would have liked to disembarrass itself of this scum by any means whatever; one felt it was on edge in all its manifestations. Drunken trams set the atmosphere ablaze. A row broke out in a café across the road. As for the prostitute who was making herself a beauty for the sixth time that night, she dropped her lipstick into the gutter. Young pupils of the "beggars' school" were making life impossible for the passers-by. Buses were rushing at a bloody speed with their cargo of unclean creatures and rotten dreams. In the air there was an imperious need for release; it was necessary that these men perish. The city demanded their death, to be able to enjoy its shameful serenity in peace.

The sweepers themselves had no inkling of the horrible diversion their presence was inflicting on the street. They merely had the order to sweep it and it had on them the effect of something dangerous and incomprehensible of which they were the docile servants. Never yet had they imagined what it would become without them, a prey to filth and dust. They did not know all their merit or to what degree the street owed to them its beautiful order and distinction. But this evening, they had all decided, it was their business not to die of hunger. For the first time in their lives these sweepers had dared, had believed themselves in a position to dare, a gesture of demand. They had the incredible, blasphemous idea of claiming their right to better existence. The three piastres a day they were paid did not suffice to let them live, not even to let them die. They had therefore demanded a half-piastre increase. With three and a half piastres a day they believed they could live more seriously. It was an idea for them, almost an ideal. And they awaited the realisation of this ideal without too much confidence, but with a wild look in their eyes. The arrival of the overseer on a bicycle would put an end to their uncertainty. This overseer on a bicycle charged with submitting their request to those in authority was to bring them a reply this evening. But the sweepers distrusted him, for he already belonged, by his rank of overseer, to another humanity, that of the oppressors. Further, they had decided that, in case of refusal they would leave him their uniforms, their brooms and the whole street.

'He shall sweep it all by himself, the son of a whore,' said a big fellow, getting to his feet; his strange accoutrement seemed like a challenge to the aesthetics of the honourable people of the city.

The creature had found no better way – to protect against the lightness of the uniforms – than to envelop himself in his wife's *milaya*. He had been an immense success with his comrades, who listened to him now as their chief. To tell the truth, this new spirit among the sweepers owed a great deal to the magnificent boldness of this man. He was a man of action, despising all kinds of authority, and whom extreme misery had taught to get his own justice. Everything in him cried out for a more solid life, and one felt in him a clearer consciousness of his own destiny and that of his companions. He was indeed the only one to move with ease in the cruel grip of that destiny. These terrified men had put all their hope in him, for he seemed to carry in his powerful hands the force which was to annihilate the torturers. 'Here it comes,' he said. He took off his *milaya* and wrapped it round his body like a broad belt. He wanted his movements to be free, for he felt battle near.

In fact, the overseer with a bicycle was arriving with the other squad of sweepers. They stopped before the shoe shop. The man in the *milaya* ordered his comrades to get up, to go and meet the overseer. The latter, holding his bicycle with

41

one hand, and in the other a slender bamboo cane, began to issue orders. But he soon realised that the sweepers were no longer obeying his injunctions, and that they were expecting something else from him. This checked him for an instant. The man in the *milaya* came up to him, tall and broad as the wave of a furious sea. He was ready for murder.

'And what have you done about us?' he demanded.

The overseer made no reply. He got on his bicycle and took his time, to prepare a brief and energetic speech. He had not forgotten that he represented authority and that a power without rival preserved him from all dangers.

'Here,' he called, 'listen, all of you. In answer to your request the administration has instructed me first of all to inform you that you are a lot of bastards. Next, that your ungrateful attitude merits the worst penalties. For it is barely a month since, in order to satisfy your dainty demands, they ruined themselves by giving you new uniforms. And today you dare to demand a rise in salary. I repeat it again and this time in my own name, you are nothing but a lot of bastards.'

What happened as a result of this discourse was atrocious and lamentable. First of all, the man in the *milaya* picked up the overseer and sent him crashing against the window of the shoe shop. The sweepers, broom in hand, stood motionless with astonishment at the sudden action of their comrade. They had no time to recover from their stupor, for already the shadow of a policeman loomed on the horizon; it was Gohloche. Soon, policemen were arriving from all sides. The battle lasted nearly a quarter of an hour during which the whole of civilisation trembled with indignation. As a crowning misfortune it was closing-time for the cinemas. What were these bastards of sweepers doing here with their dirty demands. The passers-by, replete and snug in their overcoats, were seized with disgust at this horror. They lost their optimism for several days at least. The ambulance was sent for, not for the wounded, but for a very distinguished lady who had swooned with anger on learning of the sweepers' revolt. The whole thing ended greatly to the credit of the

42

policeman Gohloche, who had given proof, in this affair, of an excessive and disinterested brutality.

The end of Black Lane was a very quiet spot. Misery dwelt there, serious misery, with a perfect equanimity of humour. It was not exacerbated by contact with an insulting luxury. Its inhabitants were not envious. They never coveted the misery of their neighbour and tried to maintain their poverty at the level of the common mean. The tinker seemed interested for a moment in the policeman and asked him for his news. Gohloche told the story of the night before and how he alone had laid out several sweepers. But he amplified his tale so much as to render it unintelligible. In any case he himself had no idea why the sweepers had hit their overseer, nor why they had conducted themselves in so unaccustomed a manner, they who were usually so modest and moderate.

'And why did they do that?' asked Chaktour.

'I cannot tell you, O man. It is a secret. You would do better to occupy yourself with your broken pot. Greetings upon you.'

'O policeman Gohloche,' cried Chaktour, 'tell me I beg you why the sweepers conducted themselves thus?'

'Upon my honour, O man, you are becoming spoilt. Have I not told you already that you were becoming spoilt? What have these sweepers to do with you?'

The policeman gone, Chaktour fell back into the thoughts that obsessed him. This revolt of the sweepers had just added to his confusion. It was now a matter of establishing a connection between two incidents of a different nature, but which he felt were provoked by the same spirit. According to him, Saadi's crime and the sweepers' revolt could only have one and the same origin.

It was necessary to close the shop. Chaktour got up and moved away, tottering a little on his legs. He was not very old. He was bent not by age but by a sort of prostration which had taken possession of his whole being, had installed itself in him like an incurable disease and which demanded a great deal of care. He collected a few remnants of tin, threw them into a corner and busied himself with putting the shop into a bit of order. He was not irked by his misery. It was vast and wide and he moved freely inside it. It was like a spacious prison: he was free to go from one wall to the other of his misery without asking anybody's permission. He was only irked by feeling it so abundant. It was a rich misery. He did not know how to spend it. He looked at the child, heir to such riches. The child was sleeping on his pile of clover; he did not seem to understand all the resources of the paternal heritage. The man woke up the child, whose lifted robe showed the young flesh where the cold came with pleasure to nibble.

'Come, little one, get up. We're going.'

The child, aroused, looked around him in the narrow shop and searched for the object of his dream. He thought he would find a sheep. He found only a lugubrious solitude that entered into his heart.

'Father,' he said. 'I'll take the clover.'

They went out into the lane. The man walked in front, revolving in his head ideas which were too great and which astonished him by the zeal with which they lived in him. The child followed, half asleep, the pile of clover under his arm. Now the lane was only lit by a few poor stars. A low and sordid sky weighed upon the roofs of the hovels and obliged them to crawl over the muddy earth. Further up, the lane lost itself in a vague open plot in the midst of which arose the huts of the ape-leader and the sorcerer. Chaktour and the child penetrated into another lane which went downhill and which led to Saroukh's café.

The man stopped and looked into the café. To his great astonishment he saw Haroussi, whom he thought in prison, seated in company with other personalities of the quarter. The restaurant-keeper had a taciturn air and was smoking his *goza* in silence; he seemed to be presiding over a funeral service. The men around him preserved an attitude full of concentration and wisdom. One could not tell what they were thinking of.

So the police had let Haroussi go. No doubt after realising that Saadi had not poisoned his wife to go to Paradise, as

44

the restaurant-keeper had advised him. So there was something else. There must be a profounder motive to the barber's crime; perhaps a quite simple one but which by reason of its very simplicity had escaped everybody's notice. This motive Chaktour wished to fathom at any price. The whole of his miserable flesh burned to discover it. It seemed to him that at the moment of this discovery he would experience as it were rest and joy. So many years of misery were lit up by the thirst of this discovery. He called Haroussi.

The restaurant-keeper came out of the café. He had the air of someone who believed himself to be the devil.

'Are you free?' asked Chaktour.

'Yes; why?'

'Come and walk a few steps with me. I want to talk to you.'

'At all events, don't ask my advice,' said Haroussi. 'I don't know how to talk any more; my tongue has been cut off!'

'Who has cut off your tongue?'

'I don't know how to answer questions any more. You saw me a moment ago sitting with those men. Well, one doesn't talk any more. From now on we are going to learn how to live without talking.'

Chaktour realised that the restaurant-keeper did not want to compromise himself any further, and that he would say nothing if he did not feel sheltered from any indiscretion. He took him by the arm and they moved towards the open plot.

The child followed them in silence. He walked, careful and sad, holding the pile of clover in his arms, and thinking at every step to meet the sheep of his dream. But, everywhere, there was nothing but wild dogs. They pullulated in this spot, attracted by the quantity of garbage and the promiscuity of men with grim and free occupations. The ape-leader had succeeded in taming some of them and had made them notorious stars. In this formless plot the obscurity was not provoked solely by the night. There was the night, but in the night one detected the presence of something else, something which was blacker than the night; the sad soul of man.

Chaktour and the restaurant-keeper stopped as soon as they saw the sky free over their heads, and sufficient space around them. One perceived, in the middle of the open patch, the sorcerer standing on the roof of his hut, devoting himself to bizarre practices. The wind whistled madly, as if it wished to chase away all this stinking misery, accumulated there over an unheard-of period. A smell of urine and dead animals dominated the whole extent of the plot; an active, overflowing smell, stronger than the winds and the years.

'Now are you going to tell me,' asked Haroussi, 'the reason for this walk? What have you got to say to me?'

'I wanted to ask you why Saadi the barber poisoned his wife.'

'I have no idea,' cried Haroussi; 'why are you asking me? Am I his father or his mother? I've had enough bad luck as it is. I want to be left alone from now on.'

He stopped and looked straight in front of him. He saw the mud, he saw the huts, he saw the sadness which arose from the earth and the greedy sky which absorbed all this sadness. He said, in a low voice which was no longer his own:

'Really, why did he poison her? Yes why?'

'You see,' said Chaktour, 'you yourself are now asking it with anguish. Soon everybody in the place will be asking it with anguish.'

'Do you know, Haroussi,' he said after a moment, 'that the sweepers have revolted and that they have hit their overseer?'

'When was this?'

'Yesterday evening. It was Gohloche the policeman who just told me.'

'And didn't he tell you why they revolted?'

'No; he told me that it is a secret and that I'd do better to mind my own business. I let him say so because he's son of a dog and he can cause me trouble. But all this seems fishy to me. I should like to know – '

'What?'

46

'What the resemblance is between Saadi's crime and the sweepers' revolt.'

'Do you think there's some connexion between the two things?'

'Not a connexion but a similar wish. A very simple wish, that I feel everywhere around me, but that I cannot identify. We need to be several to do that. All of us, with our wives and children. Then it will penetrate into our hearts, it will become terrible and it will grow in us. And when it becomes immense in us and we can no longer support its presence in our hearts, we together will commit deeds that seem senseless to us today, but which at that moment will be simple and just.'

'Are you sure?' asked Haroussi.

'Why do you ask if I'm sure? You see the child over there? You see the pile of clover? The child wanted a sheep for the holiday. I told him that we were poor. He began to cry. I thought: here I am at the bottom of misery. And then Saadi's crime came into my mind. It was torturing me, it was clinging to my body. It was at that moment that Gohloche the policeman came up and told me the story of the sweepers. I understood nothing at first. Then I tried to understand. At the bottom of my misery I felt relieved by the action of these men, and their courage gave me strength, and the taste for life woke in me. Really, how can I explain it to you? I am very old and all this was born in me this evening.'

'Chaktour my brother,' said Haroussi, 'I am just out of gaol and I am very tired, I assure you. I don't understand anything any more. But I'm going to tell you something all the same. A moment ago you showed me the child and the pile of clover to bring me nearer to your sick heart. Now in turn, look at that ape-leader down there, near his hut. See him? That is not my son; he's the son of a whore; but every time I happen to meet him, he stirs the same thought in me: Why are there no exhibitors of men? We might know then, perhaps, what men can do.'

'I know what men can do,' said Chaktour.

'Well, tell me.'

47

'I've only known it since this evening.'

'Tell me all the same.'

'Men can poison their wives, O Haroussi, they can also revolt and hit their overseer.'

'That explains nothing.'

'It explains everything. Now I see clearly, so clearly that I'm frightened. The fault is in this pile of clover. I was sleeping in my misery, smothered by it and not thinking of throwing it off. I didn't understand life without it. And then the child arrived with a pile of clover. And all of a sudden my misery became insupportable. I suffered like a man burnt alive, whose eyes have been torn out so that he cannot look around him. A pile of clover, and the way of another life was revealed to me.'

'What life?'

'I don't know how to tell you. There are things announcing themselves in the air which tell me that your blood is not utterly cold. There is still much warmth and life in us. A warmth capable of many miracles.'

'Are you going to set up as a sorcerer?'

'No, not I. Look at this child crying. He is cold, no doubt, for he is naked under his robe. He has not eaten since this morning. But he is the bearer of miracles. He is the sorcerer of tomorrow. I was asking myself just now, buried in my shop: 'Who will save the child?' Well, the child will save himself. The child will not accept this burdensome heritage of our misery. He will have arms strong enough to defend himself. That is what the air is saying around us. Listen, Haroussi . . .'

There was a silence which stretched far away, to the end of the muddy lanes. The wind had stopped blowing. The misery of the world was at the climax of its destiny.

# THE BEST CHESS PLAYER IN THE WORLD

## Julian Symons

*Julian Symons (1912– ) first achieved prominence as the editor of* Twentieth Century Verse *in the late 1930s. His first thriller was published in 1945 and he has since become Britain's most eminent contemporary crime writer. He is also a critic, historian and biographer.*

*In a country where the conservatism of the genre has been most marked, Symons has long been unusual for his progressive worldview. In the following story this is combined with his favourite subject matter, namely 'the violence behind respectable faces'. Here the respectable face belongs to an English businessman. 'The Best Chess Player in the World' was written in 1982.*

'All I ask is value for money,' George Bernard Shaw said.

The man on the other side of the desk, whose name was Roberts, shuffled his feet and looked miserable.

Shaw had been given those first names by his parents, because it was on the night of a visit to *Arms and the Man* that he had been conceived. Others might have flinched from the names, but he had accepted them even at school, and for years now had taken pleasure in using the full name, or for preference the magic initials. He regarded himself as a disciple of the original George Bernard Shaw, who in his eyes had not been a visionary socialist but a ruthless realist, fighting battles in his dealings with theatre producers, publishers, women, battles which he always won. The original Shaw had been, as he saw it, a man with cranky ideas which he cleverly exploited in plays to make himself a lot of money.

49

In life, however, he had been a logical man, and the later GBS prided himself on being logical too.

He was twenty-five when he inherited from his father a small family printing firm and a couple of weekly local papers. The local papers were now a flourishing chain of thirty, that covered the Midlands and extended up into Yorkshire and Lancashire. The printing works had enlarged with the papers.

Success had not been achieved without some difficulties, as is the way of life. There had been problems with wholesalers in some areas, people who complained that GBS gave much poorer terms than his competitors, and so refused to stock his papers. These wholesalers found their vans damaged through slashed tyres, sand in the tank, and other means. Their warehouses also suffered burglaries in which stock was damaged or destroyed. Such difficulties ceased when they handled, and pushed, GBS papers.

Then there were union problems at the works. GBS always refused to employ union members, and the local branches threatened to black him. The two union secretaries who had led the blacking movement were badly beaten up, one sustaining several broken ribs and the other a hip injury that left him permanently lame. Half a dozen other militants suffered similar, although less severe attacks, and eventually GBS's firm was left alone. He was ruler of his world, and the feeling was enjoyable. The interview with Roberts took place because it was understood that GBS was the last court of appeal. Roberts, when sacked, had gone to the top man.

'Value for money,' GBS said. 'And from the reports on the table here I'm not getting it.'

'I've been here more than twenty years.'

'Twenty-two. What then?'

'Now I'm to be turned off with a month's notice.'

'You feel you are being badly treated? Let us consider.' There was nothing he enjoyed more than an argument of this kind, in which he held all the trump cards. 'You came here and stayed here of your own free will. You worked as a packer and a machine hand, jobs that required no tradesman's skills, but still you were paid more than you would have been in a union shop. Your job, however, while involving no special skill, did demand that you should stand up at work. You tell me this is impossible – '

'It's my leg, my arthritis. You'd never believe the pain. The specialist, he says I must sit down, not all day, I got to keep moving, but just sit down sometimes, every half hour. Standing's the worst thing for it, standing all day.' Roberts was a small man with a drooping moustache. He spoke with the nasal whine of the area.

'Then of course you must sit down. But that means you are unable to do your job here.'

'I'm being thrown on the scrapheap. No pension, nothing.'

'You knew there was no pension scheme when you came – '

'I was young then, never thought about it.'

'Please do not interrupt. You should have thought, you should have saved money. Now you must look for another job.'

'With my leg, and me forty-seven years old, and unemployment what it is, what chance have I got? You could find me another job here, something behind a desk, easy enough if you wanted.'

GBS never ceased to be polite, but now he allowed his impatience to show. 'Why should I do that? The reports I have here don't suggest that you would be able to handle such work. You have never worked behind a desk, you would be useless, and we are not a charity. You must be logical, Mr Roberts. Value for money is the rule between employer and employed. If you felt you were worth more than we paid you, you were free to take another job. Now you are no longer giving value for money. What more is there to say?'

Roberts found other things to say, abusive and illogical things to which GBS paid no attention. He would not have admitted even to himself that he enjoyed such interviews, but he always found pleasure in pointing out that the value for money argument was irrefutable. The pleasure lasted during half of the forty-minute drive home. Then he began to think about Paula.

He had married Paula ten years ago, when he was thirty-five and she ten years younger. For some time he had felt no need to marry. He had a flat in the heart of the city, and when it was necessary to entertain for business purposes, a local firm sent in an excellent cook, and a maid to serve the meal. Then he had interests, apart from the firm, that kept him busy. He acknowledged the need to keep fit, and like his namesake was a useful boxer. Games seemed to him ridiculous, but he understood that they could be useful in business terms, and made himself into an efficient golfer, particularly on the greens, since putting seemed to him the most logical part of the game. He went often to race meetings, where he was a heavy punter. Was that illogical? Not so, for his bets were in the service of the Emergency Fund. When he won he was paid in cash, and the money went straight into a safe deposit account in London. This was the Emergency Fund. It had been used on several occasions when the use of cheques would have been inadvisable.

He acknowledged also the need for sex. He took girls out, sometimes for a day at the races, sometimes for dinner. Either way they ended up in bed at the flat, a result he felt essential to justify the time and money spent. A time came, however, when to his own surprise he found all this unsatisfactory. He felt the need for a house of his own, for somebody to arrange those dinners, and to sit at one end of the table. A number of business acquaintances raised their eyebrows when they found that there was no hostess at his dinners, and he knew that there were always whispers about bachelors. Then again, a good deal of trouble in the sexual line would be saved if he had a wife. It would be a practical arrangement, she would be value for money. The right kind of wife, of course, somebody who looked on marriage as logically as he did himself.

He met Paula Mountford at a party, asked her to dinner and to the theatre, but made no attempt to take her to bed. He decided that she filled the bill perfectly. She was the younger daughter of a county family that had come down in the world, good-looking enough in a slightly awkward, big-boned way, and adept in keeping her conversational end up in any sort of company. She was also a girl with an eye on the main chance, something that was evident when he took her back to the flat, kissed her, and suggested that they should get married.

'You aren't in love with me.'

'I don't talk about love, it's an abstraction. I find you attractive, and we seem to get on well.'

'Well enough,' she said coolly. She had a thick underlip, and it was stuck out now. 'I don't love you, I'm not sure that I like you very much, but you're certain of yourself, you go out for what you want, and I admire that. At the moment you seem to want me. I suppose I should be flattered.'

'I'm glad you're sensible.'

'Not much use being anything else when you're around,' she said with a laugh.

'I've got no time for romance, it seems to me nonsense. I think you should consider whether the advantages of being married to me are enough for you.'

'All right. I'll tell you what I want. A wedding in style, church not registry office, no expense spared. A house outside the city, I hate bricks and mortar all round me. An acre or so of garden. My own car, a runabout. A couple of horses, I want to keep up my hunting. Good for your image to have a wife who hunts. A big dog, retriever or a labrador. A clothes account up in London, no complaints about how much I spend. That's all at the moment, though I shall think of other things I'm sure. In return I'll grace your table and share your bed. I don't suppose you want children?' He shook his head. 'Luckily I'm not mad about them either.'

'We agree about everything. It sounds as though you're good value for money.' He smiled as he said it, but the words were serious.

'My God, you are a bastard.' She pulled him to her. He was surprised, and disconcerted, by the ardency of her embrace.

Three months later Paula Mountford became Mrs George Bernard Shaw.

For years the arrangement had, it seemed to him, worked perfectly. Paula had everything she wanted. She had chosen the house, a large modern villa out in the country with a lot of ground, and outbuildings that were converted into a stable block. She had her horses, her golden retriever. She proved to be an excellent hostess, inventive with menus, skilful in making nervous guests feel at ease. She dressed individually and with flair, and he never said a word about bills. As for sex that rather lapsed, as he felt by mutual consent. He no longer felt much need for it, and the exercise of power in the firm was something that he found much more exciting. The firm prospered, his home life prospered. He was a contented man.

Until the day when he learned that Paula had a lover.

He learned it in the simplest way. He had mislaid his cigarette lighter, looked in an old bag of hers in the hope of finding one, and there was the letter. He was an incurious man, and would not have read it except that the word 'Darling' caught his eye. The words on the page seemed to him hardly credible. Could it be Paula to whom these phrases were addressed, embarrassing and ridiculous phrases of a kind that he would never have been able to bring himself to put down on paper? Paula was up in London, and it was typical of him that his first action after making the discovery was to go on looking for a light, and then to smoke his cigarette before reading the letter again.

He congratulated himself on this calmness, but it was succeeded by a wave of anger such as he had never known. The anger had no outward manifestation, he did not break any of Paula's possessions or cut up her clothes, but the emotion shook him as he had not been shaken since he was eleven years old. He had been told then by his father that his mother had left the house forever, and gone to live with another man. He had felt that as a personal betrayal, a possession he had lost, and now he felt the same thing. Paula belonged to him, he had given her everything she ever asked for, and she had now deliberately betrayed him. She must be punished.

He made a copy of the letter, and returned it to the bag. It was, again, typical of him that he did not consider asking the name of her lover, or whether the affair was over. Such questions might lead to argument, and he only argued from a position of assured superiority. Should he employ a private detective? He decided against this, partly because it was Paula's betrayal that concerned him and not the name of her past or present lover, but principally for the reason that to consult a private detective involved putting himself to some extent in the man's power, and to put himself in somebody else's power was something that he had never done in his life. Instead he watched Paula himself, following her by car on the days when she said that she would be going out. He did not use his own car, which she might have recognised, but rented one. In less than a week he had discovered the identity of her lover. He was a man of Paula's own age, divorced from his wife, a well-to-do gentleman farmer who was a member of the hunt she rode with. The man lived a few miles away, and she went to his house one or two afternoons a week.

But GBS was little interested in the man, and did not blame him. He appreciated that to sleep with another man's wife was a kind of triumph, one he had savoured himself in his bachelor days, when the chief pleasure had been talking afterwards to the unwitting cuckold. It was Paula who must be punished, but it was easier to say this than to discover the means. He did not threaten divorce, because he feared that this would be no punishment, and also it would mean that she was no longer in his possession. What else could he do that would make her miserable as she deserved to be miserable, take away forever that look of a cat almost choked with cream that he now saw on her face? He thought about it for days while the anger grew within him, grew satisfying because he knew that it would find an outlet. Eventually he decided that the only possible punishment was death.

It was necessary to assure himself that the punishment

was just, and this was not difficult. Look at the matter logically, and it was apparent that he and Paula had an agreement. She had broken it, and no longer gave value for the money she received. It was true, and he acknowledged it, that the idea of her suffering pleased him, as he had been pleased by the lasting nature of the injuries sustained by that trade union branch secretary. He considered, and reluctantly rejected, the idea that Paula's horse face might be permanently scarred. What would happen afterwards? He could hardly divorce her without incurring blame, and he had no wish to spend the rest of his life with a disfigured woman.

He was aware that the logic he used was that of a superior man (in a phrase, the logic of GBS), and that it would not be generally understood. In the event of Paula's death he would be an obvious suspect, and he had no intention of standing in a dock, or even suffering arrest. It was essential therefore that he should not have any apparent connection with what happened. He would work through intermediaries, but none of them must see him, or be able to make a connection leading back to him. It was a difficult problem, but one of an intellectual kind, resembling a problem in chess. He played chess well, and in a day or two he had solved the problem.

The first person to see was Jerry Wilde. Jerry owed him a debt, but he would not rely on that. The logical man does not depend on emotion.

The debts Jerry owed him, for they were counted in the plural, went back to their days at grammar school. GBS had always been, like his namesake, long and wiry, physically capable of looking after himself. Jerry Wilde was the kind of perky little shrimp who was a natural target for bullying. It had been amusing to defend him, and to show his contempt for the rest of the school by making it clear that he would sooner talk to Jerry than to the captain of cricket. Jerry's worshipful attitude, his readiness to run errands and in general to do what he was told, were also agreeable. He was a lively little boy, an excellent mimic, good especially at catching the tones of other boys, and a great success in the school plays. But there was a basic dishonesty about Jerry. He would cheat in exams even though he knew the answers, and GBS had once saved him from the threat of expulsion for stealing, by pretending to find the missing money, which he had provided out of his own pocket.

Jerry's later career was much what might have been predicted. He got jobs but couldn't hold them. He went on benders and failed to turn up for work, fiddled accounts when he had anything to do with money, was always ready to help in handling TV sets, cases of whisky, or other quickly saleable things without asking where they came from. GBS had saved him from an embezzlement charge by paying his employer something over the amount Jerry had taken, and from something more serious when Jerry, blind drunk at the wheel of a car, had mounted the pavement and knocked down an old age pensioner. She had been persuaded to take money instead of pressing charges. Why did he bother with Jerry? Well, on both those occasions he had made Jerry sign a statement admitting the facts. And then Jerry seemed to know or be able to get the dirt on everybody, and GBS had made use of this knowledge. It was Jerry who had found the boys who turned the trick with the vans and those who tamed the trade unionists, who told them what to do and paid them off, so that GBS never even knew who they were. Jerry was useful.

At the moment he was working for a man who cannibalised cars, put bits and pieces into other cars that had been in accidents and sold for scrap. Then he sprayed them, changed the speedo and plates, and sold them as salesman's models.

'Looking for a car, boss? Give you a good trade-in on the one you've got.' Jerry had always been a grinner. Above the grin his nose was bright red with alcohol, his cheeks hardly less so.

'I wanted a chat.'

'Round at the King's Head?' GBS shook his head, made a gesture towards his car. 'Like that, is it? Mind the shop Bill, shan't be long.' Bill, at the back of the showroom, waved a

57

hand. They drove a couple of miles, then GBS pulled into a lay-by.

'You're going to land in trouble with those cars,' he said. 'The registration plate on that Jaguar, where did it come from?'

'Couldn't tell you off-hand.'

'And what about the registration book?'

'Looks beautiful. Don't ask where I got it, not unless you're a buyer.'

'You won't get away with it for long.'

'And when there's trouble who shall I run to? Don't tell me. Did we come out here for you to say that, or just to look at the traffic?'

'Neither. I need a little help.'

Jerry cocked his head to one side, bird-like. 'Yours to command.'

'It's a little bit like the Layton business.' Layton had sustained the hip injury.

'And you want me to find a couple of boys, fix it with them?'

'Not exactly. I want somebody reliable, very reliable. You find him, give me a number where I can call him. You don't, not on any account, mention my name. That's it.'

'That's it?' Jerry's bright bird eye showed surprise. 'You'll handle it yourself? Why and wherefore?'

'Not your business. You just give me a name and number.'

'The boss orders, it shall be done.' He sketched a salute. 'A bit ticklish though. The sort of boy I know, he knows me. But he *don't* know you, if you get my meaning. If I knew the strength of what you wanted, that would help.'

'No. It's better to stick to what I said.'

'That means it must be strong.'

He affected irritation. 'If you don't want to help, say so. There'd be fifty pounds in it for you, just for a name and number.'

'When have I ever said no? It's ticklish, that's all. I might have to put you on to somebody who'd pass you on, get me? Leave it with me for a day or two, I'll ask around. Discreetly mind, don't worry. That's it?'

'That's it.'

'Then let's get back.' When they were back at the show-room Jerry stuck his head through the car window. His breath smelt of beer and pickled onions. 'About the fifty, GBS, forget it. This one's on the house.'

Two days later he rang back with a name and number. 'Like I said, it's someone who'll make the arrangements. Can't say more, he'll tell you the rest himself. Say you're a friend of mine when you call. Ring at five o'clock any after-noon, he'll be there. And boss?'

'Yes?'

'Be careful. They're wide awake, some of these boys.'

The thought of the dangerous element involved made his blood tingle, his heart beat pleasurably faster. The danger of involvement was part of the game, its avoidance a mark of the logician's skill. Had Jerry understood that? In any case his part was now finished, and he could say nothing damaging.

He rang the number from a public call box just after five o'clock. The voice that came on was low, cautious.

'Is that Mr Middleton, Jack Middleton?'

'Yes.'

'Jerry Wilde gave me your name, said I could call you.'

'Jerry, right.'

'He thought you might be able to help me with a problem.'

'What sort of problem?'

'A friend of mine needs a job done.'

Now the voice rose a little, roughened, a voice definitely not out of the top drawer.

'I don't know what you're talking about. Who are you, what's your name?'

'My friend wants me to remain private.'

'Is that so? You just tell him my name's Jack Middleton and I like to know who I'm dealing with. Got it?'

'Yes. Don't hang up, Mr Middleton. We're talking about a big job, a lot of money.'

Silence. 'How much is a lot? And what's it for?'

'My friend wants – ' He found, quite unexpectedly, that he could not form the words. He was strongly conscious of the interior of the telephone box. On one wall somebody had written *Tony loves Lucy* and on another *United Rule OK?*.

The harsh voice said, 'What's up? Want somebody hit, is that it?'

Hit, did that mean killed? He was not sure. 'Disposed of.' The words came out choked, as if he was being strangled.

'Say it how you like. Ten grand.'

'*How* much?'

'Ten grand. That covers it, my commission included.'

He was so astonished that he was briefly silent. He wanted to expostulate, to say that the jobs done before had cost no more that a few hundred, but very likely Middleton knew nothing about them. When he found his voice he said, 'That's much more than my friend expected. It's too much.'

'Please yourself. That's the price.'

'I must – must consult. I take it nothing would be payable until – '

'Half in advance, other half when it's done.'

'But that would be trusting you with five thousand pounds.'

'Who's trusting who, mister?' the coarse voice asked. 'I don't even know your bloody name.'

He left the box a little shaken. He was so used to being in a position of mastery, to dealing with everybody as he had dealt with Roberts, that to be almost in the position of a supplicant was disconcerting. Perhaps he should give up the whole thing, tell Paula that he knew of her affair and threaten to cut off her allowance and stop her charge accounts? But supposing she ignored him, supposing she went off to live with her gentleman farmer and made him a laughing stock? Even the possibility was not to be contemplated.

That weekend they gave a dinner party. The food was delicious, Paula as usual an admirable hostess, but he felt half a dozen times during the evening that she was mocking him. When the guests had gone he felt such a wave of fury that he could have strangled her, or shot her with the old

Webley that he had inherited from his father, who had fancied himself as a shot and had set up a target in the back garden. In fact the revolver was in his desk drawer and they were talking in the bedroom, so that the question of such a spontaneous action did not arise. In any event it would of course have been stupid, illogical, unworthy of GBS. But that evening made him decide to go ahead. On Monday evening he rang Middleton again, calling as he had been told to do at five o'clock.

'I've talked to my friend. He'd like to go ahead. On the lines you mentioned.'

'What's his name? Your *friend*, I mean.'

'No names. That's a condition.'

'All right.' There was an unexpected chuckle. 'But there's one name you gotta give me, what you might call the subject.' GBS gave Paula's name, and their address. 'You never said it was a woman.'

He replied with a touch of his usual acerbity. 'Before we were just talking. Now it's serious, and there are things I want to know. Is your agent reliable? Does it make any difference to him that it's a woman?'

'Makes no odds to him, it's just a job. He was one of those what you call 'em, mercenaries, out in Angola, freelance now. You can talk to him yourself, make up your own mind.'

'I don't want to meet him.'

'You don't have to. I said talk, not meet. I'll give you a number to ring, ask for Charlie.'

'About making payment – '

'Talk to Charlie. You fix it with him, you pay him, he gives me my cut. He knows there might be a job, so just mention me. Here's the number.' He gave it. 'Just one thing, he ain't always there. I'd call in the evening, between six and eight. After eight he's usually out with the boys.'

'He's reliable, he wouldn't talk about it to them?'

'He's a professional.'

The first time he rang the number there was no reply. The second time a voice answered, and said it was Charlie.

'I've been put on to you by Jack Middleton. About a job I want done.'

'Jack said something, gave me the name. And you're Mr X, incognito you might call it.' The voice had a disagreeable twang to it, some accent he could not place. Was it South African? Charlie began asking practical questions. When did he want it done? As soon as possible. GBS had given some thought to the method, and said that if it could look like a car accident, that would be ideal. Charlie said a decisive no to that, as too hard to arrange. Then an attempted burglary of the house, the subject came home unexpectedly –

The voice with its odd twang interrupted. 'You've been reading too many books, Mr X. First thing I look after is Number One. It's got to be simple, probably at night, a gun with a silencer. If I can make it look like a robbery okay, but don't rely on it. Don't rely on anything, except the job being done.'

'When?'

'Give me a week after I've got the first instalment. Let's talk about that. I want used notes, ones and fives. You drop it by a rubbish bin on the London road, I pick it up, I'll give you the details.'

'No.'

For the first time the voice lost its assurance. 'What you mean, no?'

'That won't do. You could check on my car or see me. You said I'm incognito. I want to stay that way. Now, this is what I propose . . .'

Charlie listened, then said, 'And the other five? When the job's done?'

'The same way.'

'Fancy but clever. Think of everything, Mr X, don't you?'

'I try to.' Then they discussed the timing.

The conversation took place on Monday evening. On Wednesday afternoon GBS took the 2.30 train out of the city. It was a slow train that stopped at several places, and it was busy during the rush hours but two-thirds empty in the

62

afternoons, so that he had no trouble in finding a carriage to himself.

When he was a boy they had lived at Thelsby, almost at the end of the line, and he had travelled hundreds of times on the train to school. A couple of miles before Thelsby there was a stretch of single-track line, and the train from the city always stopped to let one from the other direction come through. At the point where it stopped there was a grass embankment to one side, and often in that distant past he and Jerry had jumped out of the carriage, half-run and half-rolled down the grass, leapt down the steep bank at the end, and wriggled through the wire that separated the embankment from the road.

Today the train stopped as it had always done. GBS muffled his face in a scarf. There was a whistle, the train for the city passed them. He opened the carriage window. Their own train began to move, very slowly. He flung the cheap attaché case as far as he could down the grass slope. He could see no sign of Charlie, who was no doubt concealed behind the steep drop at the bottom. All Charlie could have seen of him was a hand, and a face hidden behind a scarf. On the way back from Thelsby he looked out to where he had thrown the attaché case, and saw only grass.

It was perfect.

He recited the perfection of it to himself all the way home. It was inevitable that after Paula's death all three people involved, Jerry, Jack and Charlie, should assume that he had ordered it. Let them think so, for they could prove nothing. And what could the police prove? If they talked to Jerry, any admission he made would be damaging to himself, and so could be ruled out. As for Jack Middleton and Charlie, what identification could they make beyond a voice on the telephone?

Of course he would be a suspect. He was prepared for long interrogations, and even looked forward to them because he knew that he would emerge triumphant. No doubt the police would discover the gentleman farmer, but this revelation would come as a total surprise to GBS. (How wise he had been not to use a private detective.) And the police would look in vain for any discrepancies in his bank account, or any large withdrawals, for the money had come from the Emergency Fund. Would he pay the rest of the money after the job was done? He kept an open mind about it, feeling that it must be possible to make some deal with Charlie.

It was a logical operation, and in such an operation every possibility is taken into account, so that the unexpected cannot occur. He had only to sit back and await the result.

Thursday passed, and Friday. He drove into the works as usual, chaired editorial discussions, had talks with a consortium that was talking about making an offer for two of his weeklies. While he went about these occupations he waited for the telephone call, or for the policeman who would begin: 'I'm sorry to say, Mr Shaw, that . . .' On Friday afternoon, he knew, Paula saw her farmer. Perhaps while she was driving home . . . or when she returned to the house. . . ?

But when he returned on Friday he was greeted by the smell of boeuf bourguignon and found Paula in the kitchen, making a first course of avocado and prawns. She had the *sleek* look she always wore after a session with her lover, a look that dissipated any possible feeling of regret. On Saturday Paula went out with the hunt, on Sunday morning the papers were late and she drove down to the village to get them. Each time he wound himself up into a state of expectation, but nothing happened. On Sunday evening he was unable to sit still to watch TV, made an excuse and went to his study, where he sat at his desk staring out into the dark night. When he returned she was watching a gangster series.

On Monday morning she said that she was going to London. Whether she did so, or saw her farmer, she was at home in the evening.

On Tuesday nothing happened.

*Give me a week after I've got the first instalment.* On Wednesday afternoon the week was up. And on that evening Paula came home in the best of spirits after, as she said, an afternoon spent with a couple of girl friends. They were giving a dinner party on Friday, and she had done some shopping for it.

On Thursday morning he left home as usual, went to a call box and rang Charlie's number. No reply. He drove in to the works, dealt with correspondence, went out twice to call boxes. The number rang, but there was no answer. Ring between six and eight in the evening, Jack Middleton had said. He rang at six with no result, and then called the exchange to ask if the line was in working order. In less than a minute the operator came back to him.

'That number is a public call box.'

'*What?* It isn't possible. There must be a mistake.'

'I will repeat the number,' the operator said, and did so. 'Is that correct? Very good. That is the number of a public call box.'

He asked where it was, and was given the name of a street in the east end of the city. He drove down there, looked at the red glass-windowed box, even went into it as though there might be an answer to his questions within. In some way or other he had been cheated, either by Charlie or by Jack Middleton. He did not ring Middleton, but went to see Jerry Wilde.

Jerry was in the King's Head, drinking what was obviously not his first or second brandy and soda. He greeted GBS with a slap on the back, and asked how things were going.

'I have to talk to you. Come out now. Right away.'

'Can't be done, boss. Got to meet a man about a car. Big deal. Be here any minute. Then taking him out for a drive, back here, have a couple of drinks, argue the toss about the price – '

It might just have been possible to talk sense to Jerry now, but in an hour or two it would be useless to try.

'Come and see me tomorrow.'

'Anything you say. When and where?'

On Friday there was a meeting at the office which was likely to take all day. He told Jerry to come to the house at six o'clock. He would be gone long before seven-thirty, when the dinner party guests arrived.

'Unexpected honour, boss. I'll be there.' It was true that Jerry was not the kind of person he asked home, and that Paula did not care for him, but the circumstances were exceptional.

On Friday, punctually at six, Jerry drove up in a Jaguar, no doubt the one with the fake registration book. He wore a hat with a little feather in it, and a check suit. Paula was passing through the hall on the way to the kitchen when he arrived, and greeted him coolly. After that they went to the study. GBS sat behind his desk and told Jerry what had happened. At the end he said, 'I want an explanation.'

Jerry wriggled. 'You know what you sound like? Old Porson, our old head. *I want an explanation, Wilde*. And I knew I'd never be able to explain, not to his satisfaction. You wouldn't have a drink handy?'

'After the explanation.'

'I only put you in touch with Jack Middleton. Have you tried ringing him?'

'No. It was Charlie who arranged to take the money.'

'Trouble is I don't know Charlie, do I? Why not try Jack, see what he's got to say? Here, I'll dial the number for you, I know it.' He did so, and held up the receiver so that GBS could hear the ringing tone. Then he dialled again.

'What are you doing?'

'Just checking. Operator, will you run a check on one-eight-three-four-six. I've been dialling, and can't get a reply. What's that, what do you say? Well I never. Many thanks.' He put down the telephone, grinned. 'Would you believe it, that's a public call box.'

'But that isn't possible. You put me in touch with Middleton.'

'That's right.'

'You must know him.'

'Right again, boss, I know him.' Out of Jerry Wilde's grinning face came the rough voice. *'You just tell him my name's Jack Middleton*. I know Charlie too.' And GBS heard again that disagreeable twang. *'You've been reading too many stories,*

*Mr X. The first thing I look after is Number One.* I was always able to manage voices, remember?'

Even now he could not believe it. 'The attaché case. It was you who collected it.'

'Nobody else. I thought it was a nice touch, dropping it where we used to scramble down as kids. Sentimental. Nearly piped my eye.'

'You've robbed me, stolen five thousand pounds.'

Jerry's grin became a laugh. 'I don't see it that way. I reckon you owe it me.'

'But I've always helped you. I kept you out of prison.'

'And made me sign statements so that you could hold 'em over me. Only you can't use 'em now, can you, or you'd have to say why you hung on to them so long. Did you think I liked being a errand boy? Anyway, the answer's no. So when you were so mysterious I thought, well, let's see just what he's got in mind, shall we. And my word, wasn't it naughty?' Jerry wiped his red face with a handkerchief, and went on.

'I wouldn't try again to do something naughty about your wife, because I might have something interesting to tell the fuzz. And you can't do anything about the five thousand, can you, *boss?* I'm taking a holiday for a few weeks, can't make up my mind whether it's Madeira or the West Indies, but before I went I wanted to see your face when I told you. Incidentally, I bet you meant to cheat poor old Charlie out of his second five grand. Do you know where I'd say you are, boss? Up the creek without a paddle.'

Before this speech was half-way through, George Bernard Shaw had ceased to be a logical and reasonable man, and had become a machine filled with nothing but hatred for the creature opposite him. He acted not reasonably, but from this uncontrollable hatred, when he opened the right hand drawer of the desk, took out the revolver, and shot Jerry Wilde neatly between the eyes.

George Bernard Shaw went to Broadmoor. There he became the chess champion, and every month composed a chess problem which he sent to the world champion, challenging him to solve it. From the fact that he never received any reply to these communications he made the logical deduction that the champion was unable to solve the problems, and by the extension of this logic that George Bernard Shaw was the best chess player in the world.

# I SPY

## Joan Smith

*Joan Smith (1953– ) lives in Oxfordshire. A former* Sunday Times
*journalist, she is the author of two crime novels,* A Masculine
Ending *and* Why Aren't they Screaming?. *She has also written
a book about Britain's nuclear weapons test in the 1950s,* Clouds
of Deceit, *and her latest book,* Misogynies, *is a series of reflections
on the subject of woman-hating.*

*'I Spy' is a thriller showing the British secret state at work. It is
published here for the first time.*

'And those are her exact words – someone's trying to kill
me?'

'Yes. It's hardly the sort of thing I'm likely to forget, is it?'

'No, I meant – what I meant was, she didn't say, *I think*
someone's trying to kill me? She was definite about it?'

'Very.' Mick finished his drink and held the empty glass
up in front of her. 'Another one?'

Janet looked anxiously at her watch. 'I don't know, I'm
late already . . . I did promise to do the cooking tonight –
God, I don't know what to do. This is a bit of a bombshell
– especially after last week . . .'

'Exactly. Look, are you sure you haven't got time for
another one? This *is* important.'

Janet sighed and looked distractedly round the pub. 'All
right. Just a – a tomato juice will do.'

'All the trimmings?'

She waved her hand impatiently in the air. 'It doesn't
matter. As it comes.'

She watched Mick walk to the bar, then dropped her gaze

to the table and began tracing patterns on its damp surface with her index finger. She did not look up again until Mick placed a glass of tomato juice in front of her, when she reached out automatically and drew it nearer.

'What did you say?' she asked suddenly.

'Nothing. You were lost in thought.'

'Not *now*. When she – announced all this.'

'Ah. I think I said – nothing very profound. What I actually said was – sorry? And she repeated it.'

'And did she say . . . who it is – this person who's trying to kill her?'

'Nope. I think she thought it was obvious. After last week.'

'Shit.'

'You can say that again.'

Janet shifted uncomfortably in her seat and took a sip of her drink. 'Well, we knew she might be difficult when we decided to publish her stuff.'

'Difficult! I'm not sure that's what I'd call it. Being temperamental is one thing, but this – '

'OK, OK. I suppose you're about to remind me you were against her writing for the magazine in the first place.'

'No, but since you've mentioned it . . .'

'But even you didn't expect this.'

'Good God no. All I'd heard was she could make life difficult for other people, especially anyone who has an interest in what she regards as her territory. I thought she might be – disruptive. Which, you have to admit, is true. She hit the roof when Dick came in with that story about cruise missile transporters.'

'Yes.' Janet smiled briefly. 'You handled her very well, I thought.'

'Thank *you*, ma'am.' Mick dropped his head in a mock bow.

'No, I meant – '

'It's all right, Janet. It's no secret that I'm not your choice of deputy editor. But since I was here when you arrived – '

Janet's cheeks went red. 'Mick, I've never had any doubts about your ability as a journalist . . .'

'Nor I yours.' Mick smiled, then looked serious again. 'But that's not what we're here to talk about. D'you know, until this happened, I was beginning to change my mind about her? I know she hasn't had much time at the magazine, but the stuff she's come up with, it's . . . fantastic. And it checks out – yes, I know you're not going to like this, but I did make a few calls on the first couple of stories she brought in. I'd heard – well, a mate of mine on that little magazine she wrote for in Wales, the green anarchist thing, he said they weren't sure how reliable she was. Once or twice they nearly ended up with egg on their faces. So I just made a few checks, as far as you can check these things. And it was the goods.'

'You had absolutely no right to do that.' Janet had gone white with anger.

'I was only thinking of the magazine.' Mick gave her a frank, open look. 'I've put six years of my life into it, more if you count the stuff I did as a freelance, and – well, come on, Janet, we can't afford to take risks. There's nothing the government would like better than to see us make complete fools of ourselves. Thatcher's got the rest of the press where she wants them, ready to lick her arse every time she bends over – sorry, but it's true,' he added, seeing Janet's frown.

'It was actually your imagery I was objecting to,' Janet said curtly, running one hand through her short brown hair and setting her ear-rings swinging. 'Do you have to be sexist?'

'Sexist? Christ, Janet – ' Mick stopped and grinned. 'You've got to remember, I'm an unreconstructed old chauvinist. A left-over from the sixties. All this feminist stuff is new to me. I'm sorry, OK?' He picked up his beer and swallowed a considerable quantity of Bass.

'I – all right. So the problem, as you see it, is that I've agreed to take stuff from an inexperienced journalist with a pretty good track record on alternative magazines – '

'Absolutely. I'm not denying that.'

' – but whose behaviour in the last week seems to suggest that she might be a bit of a . . . a fantasist?'

'That's a fair summary.'

71

'OK, let's go back to last week. When she said – when she told you she used to work for MI5, did she give you any . . . evidence?'

Mick grinned. 'Like what? Her membership card? I don't think the intelligence service has got round to issuing identity cards yet.'

'No, but was there anything – any circumstantial evidence? Did she give you any details?'

'She said she'd been recruited at university, just before she took her finals. Unprovable, but also quite plausible, given her subject and where she did her degree.'

'Did she say why she was telling you that she – that she'd been recruited?'

'Well, as I think I told you at the time, she thought I'd already guessed. Maybe she'd heard I'd been making a few checks on her stories. Anyway, she was quite casual about it. We were the last people left in the office, and I was just asking her how she was settling down, whether she was enjoying writing for the magazine. And she suddenly said – "You've guessed, haven't you?" And I said, guessed what? And she said – '

'All right, this is beginning to sound like a game of consequences . . . Look, you told me last week you were half inclined to believe her.'

'Yes. At the time I was. I mean, her contacts are so good. And she's very mysterious about them. In a funny sort of way, I could see it made sense. But, if you remember, I also said I was worried about the other possibility.'

'That she was making it up, you mean?'

'That. But I also wondered if she was only half telling the truth.'

Janet looked at him blankly.

'Think about it. If MI5 did want to infiltrate someone into the office, what better way to do it than send someone posing as a left-wing journalist? She gets a few scoops, fed to her very carefully and designed to make a stink without doing any real harm. Like her story about those revised NATO plans. I know Labour made a great fuss about them, but does it really matter? Did anything get changed?'

'Not that time, but – ' Janet stopped, biting her lip.

'What's the matter?'

'Nothing. Go on.'

'All right.' Mick looked at Janet curiously for a moment, then continued. 'Meanwhile, she has access to the entire office. She could be there now, updating MI5's files on all of us – what everyone's working on, who's fiddling their expenses even. Which reminds me, I need to talk to you about Andrew, but never mind that for the moment. She bides her time, then she comes up with some amazing scoop and drops us in the shit. A big libel case, maybe, the sort of thing that would finish the magazine off. Or some great big story which seems plausible but turns out, after we've published it of course, not to be true. You know the sort of thing. And you know the state of the magazine's finances. It couldn't stand that sort of scandal. Our readers have to be able to trust us. What's wrong?'

Janet's face was pinched and pale. 'She's been working on something for a couple of weeks – she's got this story – well, it's big. It could – I mean, this is the biggie.'

Mick stared at her. 'I don't know anything about this.'

'No.' Janet avoided his gaze. 'We decided – she and I – that the fewer people who knew about it the better.'

'Even your own deputy? You really don't trust me.' There was a note of resignation in Mick's voice.

Janet gave him an anguished look. 'I know how it must seem. I'm *sorry*. It's just such an amazing story – if true.'

'You mean you're not sure?'

'Well, I was . . . But now – I mean, why didn't she come to me about all this? We talked on Tuesday afternoon, after the editorial meeting, and she never mentioned any of it. In fact, I was waiting . . . that's why I asked to see her, to give her a chance to tell me what she'd told you last week. But she didn't.'

'Maybe she's telling different stories to different people. What is it, by the way, this big exclusive?'

73

Janet glanced nervously round the pub. 'You can't expect me to tell you here.'

'Come on, the place is almost empty.' Mick's gaze swept round the dingy room. 'We're the only customers under the age of 80. You're not telling me that the old girl – sorry, woman – in the corner is a secret agent?'

Janet shook her head. 'I can't. It's too risky.'

'Christ, look at what she's doing to us! If you and I can't trust each other – '

'It's not that . . .'

'OK, OK, I'm not going to press you.'

There was silence for a moment as Janet stared unseeingly ahead. Then she turned back to Mick, her tone half accusing. 'But you did say . . . last week, you were inclined to believe her.'

'Well, I didn't think it was absolutely implausible, as I just said. This, on the other hand . . .'

'Did she give you any details? She must have said what made her think – why she believes – someone's trying to kill her.'

'Oh, something about how she thought she was being followed. And the seat in her car being loose.'

'The seat in her car?'

'She said she got in her car and the seat shot backwards. The bolts had been loosened, something like that. It was all very vague.'

Janet stared at him for a moment, then took another sip of her drink. 'It doesn't sound very – oh God, this is terrible.'

'I know. The question is, what are you going to do about it?'

'Me?'

Mick shrugged. 'You're the editor. And at a time like this, I must say I'm very glad I'm not in your shoes.'

Janet sighed. 'What would you do?'

'It isn't up to me. I'm not the editor.'

'There's no need to keep saying that.'

'But it's true. The buck stops with you.'

'All right! But you could at least – talk it over with me.'

'I thought that's what we were doing.'

'Well, I suppose . . . d'you think I should speak to her?'

'Do you?'

'I – I don't know. If she tells me the same story . . . we're not much farther ahead. Or she might deny it – '

'In which case you'll have to decide who to believe – her or me.'

'Oh, don't be silly.' Janet waved her hand impatiently. 'As you say, you've been with the magazine for years. There's no contest. But if I don't talk to her . . . I suppose I can publish or not publish.'

'Is it checkable?'

'No. I can't really explain, not without going into detail . . . but in the end it's her word about what someone said, and where some documents come from – ' Janet shook her head miserably.

'So if she isn't telling the truth . . .'

Janet shrugged.

'On the other hand, if she is – you've got a sensational story.'

'So I thought. God, this is all so difficult. Mick, what am I going to do?'

Mick said nothing.

'I mean, if I decide to – to tell her I'm not going to use it, she'll be furious, you know what she's like. She'll probably go straight to someone else and offer them the story. Though I doubt if anyone else would run it – I suppose there is that consolation. As you say, Thatcher's got the press where she wants it.'

'Well, they'd have to make exactly the same decision,' Mick said shortly. 'Is she a bloody good journalist, or is she a fantasist? It's an occupational hazard, of course.'

'What is?'

'Investigative journalism. I remember years ago, when I was just starting out, I used to know this bloke on one of the Sundays. Wonderful reputation, but when I was doing some subbing shifts I found out they only ran half of what he wrote – and that was checked by two other people. He was a conspiracy theorist, you see – he'd begun seeing plots in the most extraordinary places. Half the time he was right, of course. Trouble was, the other half he wasn't. But they could afford him, they had the staff. To do the checking.'

'And we can't.'

Mick shrugged. 'I've told you, it's up to you. You've got to decide.'

'What if I get it wrong?'

'That's the risk you have to take. But I'll tell you this, if it makes it any easier. I'm with you, whatever you decide. Either way. We have to put up a united front.'

'Thanks. But you won't say – what you'd do.'

'No. It's up to you.'

Janet put down her glass. 'I haven't any choice. I'll tell her' – she took a deep breath – 'I'll tell her on Monday. I'm not going to run the story. If she takes it badly – we'll just have to live with that.'

Mick said nothing. Janet began pulling on her coat.

'I'm – I'm very grateful,' she said, standing up. 'I'll speak to you on Monday. After I've told her.' She swung the strap of her bag over her right shoulder. 'See you then.'

She hesitated, then walked briskly to the door with the air of someone buoyed up by the knowledge that she has just made a difficult decision. Mick looked at his watch, took out an evening paper, and began to glance idly through it. A few minutes later he got up, leaving the newspaper folded on the table, and walked out of the pub.

Outside in the dark street it had begun to drizzle. Mick turned up the collar of his shabby overcoat and walked towards the old-fashioned red telephone kiosk which stood in the shadow of a railway bridge at the end of the street. He pulled open the door, stepped inside, and felt in his pocket for a handful of change. He inserted three coins and punched in a number.

'Personnel.' A man's voice, accentless, non-committal.

Mick smiled to himself. 'The employee in question is leaving the company,' he said softly. 'Disciplinary action will no longer be necessary.'

76

'Thank you for letting us know,' the voice said. 'A most satisfactory solution for everyone concerned.'

The phone clicked and Mick replaced the receiver, not bothering to retrieve the unused money which clattered noisily into the returned coins slot. He pushed backwards to open the heavy swing door, glanced quickly along the street, then stepped out into the damp November night. Whistling softly, he buried his hands deep in the pocket of his overcoat and began to walk in the direction of the nearest tube station.

# THE COLLECTOR

## Rubem Fonseca

*Rubem Fonseca (1932– ) is a leading Brazilian writer. His crime fiction includes the private eye novel* A Grande Arte *(published in English as* High Art*) and short stories in the collections* A Coleira do Cao *and* O Cobrador – *from which 'The Collector' is taken. This is the – highly disturbing – story of a man under pressure from a system which excludes him. It is published here for the first time in English. The translation is by John and Tereza Rogers.*

On the front door a large set of false teeth, below it written 'Dr Carvalho, Dentist'. In the empty waiting room a sign *'Wait for the Doctor, he is attending a client'*. I waited half an hour, my tooth aching; the door opened and a woman appeared accompanied by a large fellow, roughly forty, in a white jacket.

I went in to the consulting room, sat down in the chair, the dentist placed a paper napkin around my neck. I opened my mouth and said that my back tooth was aching a lot. He looked at it with a small mirror and asked how I could have let my teeth get into that state.

You've got to laugh. These guys are funny.

I will have to extract it, he said, you already have few enough teeth and if you don't get treatment soon you will lose all the others, including these here – and he rapped my front teeth sharply.

An anaesthetic injected into the gums. He displayed the tooth with the forceps: The root is rotten, see? he said lightly. That's four hundred cruzeiros.

You've got to laugh. Ain't got it, mate, I said.

Ain't got what?

Ain't got four hundred cruzeiros. I started walking towards the door.

He blocked the doorway with his body. You'd better pay, he said. He was a large man with large hands and strong wrists from so much pulling of poor bastards' teeth. Also, my frail build encourages people. I hate dentists, shopkeepers, lawyers, industrialists, civil servants, doctors, executives, all that scum. They're all owing me a lot. I opened my jacket, took out the .38, and spoke in such a rage that a drop of spittle hit him in the face – What if I stuff this up your arse? He paled, backed away. Aiming the revolver at his chest I began to relieve the feelings in my heart: I pulled drawers out of cabinets, threw everything on the floor, kicked all the glass vials as if they were balls, popping and exploding against the wall. Tearing down the spittoons and motors was more difficult, I even hurt my hands and feet. The dentist looked at me, must have thought several times about jumping on me, I very much wanted him to do just that so that I could shoot that big belly full of shit.

I'll never pay anything again, I'm tired of paying, I shouted at him, now I only collect.

I shot him in the knee. Should have killed that son of a bitch.

The street full of people. I tell myself and sometimes the outside world that everybody owes me something. They owe me food, pussy, blanket, shoes, house, car, watch, teeth, that's what they are owing me. A blind man goes begging and shakes some coins in an aluminium cup. I kick out at his cup, the rattling of coins irritates me. Marechal Floriano Street, gunshop, pharmacy, bank, chinashop, portrait artist, Electricity Board, innoculations, doctor, Ducal department store, hordes of people. In the morning, you can't walk towards the Central station, the masses sweep along like an enormous caterpillar occupying the whole pavement.

These Mercedes owners irritate me. The car horn also annoys

me. Last night I went to see the guy in the Cruzada who had a Magnum with silencer for sale and when I was crossing the street, a bloke who had gone to play tennis in one of those smart clubs they have around there blew his horn. Because I was thinking about the Magnum, I wasn't paying attention when the horn blew. I saw that the car was coming slowly and stopped in front of it.

What are you up to? he shouted.

It was night time and there was no one near. He was dressed in white. I pulled out the .38 and fired at the windscreen, more to shatter the glass than to get him. He accelerated the car, so as to hit me or to escape, or both. I jumped to one side, the car drove past with its tyres hissing on the asphalt surface. It stopped nearby. I went there. The bloke was lying down with his head back, face and chest covered with thousands of small slivers of glass. He was bleeding heavily from an ugly wound in his throat and his white clothes were already totally red.

He turned his head, which was resting on the car seat, eyes wide open, black, and the surrounding white was milky blue, like the inside of a jabuticaba. It was because the white of his eyes were bluish that I said – are you going to die, mate, do you want me to put you out of your misery?

No, no, he said with effort, please.

I saw a fellow watching me from the window of a building. He hid when I looked. He must have phoned the police.

I walked away calmly and returned to the Cruzada. It had been great to shatter the Mercedes' windscreen. I should have fired a shot at the bonnet and one into each of the doors, the bodywork repairer would have had a busy time.

The guy with the Magnum had already returned. Where are the thirty thousand? Put them here in this little hand that has never been beaten, he said. His hand was white, smooth, but mine was full of scars, my whole body is scarred, even my dick is covered with scars.

I want to buy a radio as well, I said to the spiv.

Whilst he went to get the radio I looked carefully at the

Magnum. Well oiled and also loaded. With its silencer, it looked like a cannon.

The spiv came back carrying a battery radio. It's Japanese, he said.

Switch it on so I can hear the tone.

He switched it on.

Louder, I asked.

He increased the volume.

Phut. I think he died instantly from the first shot. I fired another two shots just to hear phut, phut.


They owe me college, girlfriend, hifi, respect, mortadella sandwich at the bar in Vieira Fazenda Street, ice cream, a football.

I stay in front of the TV to build up my hate. When my rage is decreasing and I lose the urge to collect what they owe me, I sit in front of the TV and my hate returns in a short time. I very much want to get a certain individual who makes a whisky advert. He's all nicely dressed, very good looking, all sanforised, embracing a luscious blonde, and he drops ice cubes into a glass and smiles with all his teeth, his teeth are all perfect and they're real, and I want to get him with a razor and slit the two sides of his cheeks to his ears, and then those white teeth will all be out in the smile of a red skull. Now he's there, smiling, and then kisses the blond on the lips, There's nothing to be lost by waiting.

My arsenal is almost complete: I have a Magnum with silencer, a Cobra Colt .38, two razors, a 12-bore carbine, a Taurus .38 sawn-off shotgun, a dagger and a machete. With the machete I'm going to cut off someone's head in one single stroke. I saw in the cinema, in one of those Asiatic countries, still during the period of the British, a ritual that consisted of cutting off the head of an animal, a buffalo I think, in a single stroke. The British officers were presiding over the ceremony with an air of boredom, but the executioners were true artists. A clean stroke and the animal's head rolled, the blood spurting.

82

In the home of a woman who picked me up in the street. Old hag, says she studies at evening class. I've already gone through this, my college was the most nocturnal of all the night classes in the world, so bad that it doesn't exist any more, it was demolished. Even the street in which it was has been demolished. She asks what I do and I say that I am a poet, which is strictly true. She asks me to recite one of my poems. Here it is: The rich like to sleep late/only because they know the vermin/have to sleep early to work in the morning/This is another chance that they/have to be different:/to be a parasite,/to despise those who sweat to earn their food,/to sleep late/late/one day/hopefully too much.

She interrupts, asking if I like the cinema. What about the poem? She doesn't understand. I continue: You knew how to samba and to fall in love/and to roll on the floor/only for a short time./From the sweat of your brow, nothing has been built/you wanted to die with her,/but this was another day,/yet another day./In the Iris cinema, in Carioca street/the Phantom of the Opera/ a person in black,/black case, his face hidden,/an immaculate white handkerchief in his hand,/frigging the spectators;/during the same period, in Copacabana,/another/without even a nickname,/drank the piss from the cinema's urinals/and his face was green and unforgettable./History is made by dead people/and the future of people who are going to die./Do you think she will suffer?/She's strong, she'll resist./She would resist as well, if she had been weak./Now I don't know about you./You pretended for so long, fought and shouted, swindled./You're tired,/you're finished,/I don't know what keeps you alive.

She didn't understand poetry. She was alone with me and wanted to pretend indifference, giving exasperated yawns. The farce of women.

I'm scared of you, she finally admitted.

This old hag doesn't owe me anything, I thought, she lives with difficulty in a one-bedroom flat, her eyes are already swollen from drinking rubbish and reading about the life of high-society women in *Vogue* magazine.

Do you want me to kill you? I asked whilst we were drinking cheap whisky.

I want you to fuck me, she laughed anxiously, in doubt.

Should I finish her off? I had never strangled anyone with my own hands. Strangling someone hasn't got much style, or drama, it's like a street fight. Even so I had the urge to strangle someone, but not a miserable one like her. For a nobody, will only a shot in the back of the head do?

I have been thinking about this, recently. She had taken off her clothes: shrivelled and flat breasts, the nipples large raisins that someone had trodden on; flaccid thighs spotted with cellulitis, spoilt jelly with pieces of rotten fruit.

I'm shivering, she said.

I lay on her. She held me round the neck, her mouth and tongue in my mouth, her vagina clammy, hot and odorous.

We fucked.

She is sleeping now.

I'm fair.


I read the newspapers. The death of the spiv from the Cruzada hasn't even been mentioned. The slick guy with the Mercedes in tennis kit died in Miguel Couto Hospital and the papers said that he had been attacked by the bandit Boca Large. You've got to laugh.

I write a poem called Childhood or New Smells of a Pussy with a U: Here am I again/listening to the Beatles/on Radio Mundial/ at nine o'clock at night/in a bedroom/that could be/and was/of a mortified saint/I had not sinned/and I don't know why they shunned me like a leper/because I was innocent/or an ass/At any rate/the ground was always there/for diving./When you have no money/it's good to have muscles/and hate.

I read newspapers to know what they are eating, drinking and doing. I want to live long enough to have time to kill them all.


From the road I watch the party in Vieira Souto Street, the women in long dresses, the men in dark clothes. I walk slowly, from one side of the pavement to the other, I don't want to arouse suspicion and the machete inside my trousers, strapped to my leg, doesn't allow me to walk properly. I look like a cripple, I feel a cripple. A middle-aged couple pass me by and look at me pityingly; I also feel sorry for myself, I limp and feel the pain in my leg.

From the pavement I see the waiters serving French champagne. These people like French champagne, French dresses, the French language.

I had been there since nine o'clock, when I had been passing by, all armed, a hostage to fortune and to bad luck, and the party materialised.

The parking spaces in front of the apartment were immediately filled and the cars of the visitors began to be parked in the dark side streets. One of these interested me a lot, a red car and in it a man and a woman, young and elegant. They walked to the building without exchanging a word, he adjusting his bow tie and she her dress and hair. They prepared for a triumphal entrance but from the pavement I see that their arrival was, like that of the others, received with lack of interest. People do themselves up at the hairdressers, at the dressmaker, at the beauty parlour and, at the parties, it is only their mirror that gives them the attention they hope for. I saw the woman in her flickering blue dress and murmured – I am going to give you the attention that you deserve, it wasn't for nothing that you wore your best panties and went so many times to the dressmaker and spread so many creams on your skin and used such expensive perfume.

They were the last to leave. They did not walk with the same purpose and discussed irritatedly, their voices husky, confused.

I got near them as the man opened the car door. I was limping and he only gave me a glance in rapid evaluation, seeing an inoffensive cheap cripple.

I pushed the revolver into his back.

Do what I tell you or I kill you both, I said.

To get into the narrow back seat with a stiff leg wasn't easy. I stayed half-crouched, the revolver pointing at his head. I told him to head for Barra da Tijuca. I took out the machete from inside my trouser leg when he said, take the money and the car and leave us here. We were in front of the Hotel Nacional. You've got to laugh. He was already sober and wanted to have a last whisky as he complained to the police by phone. Ah, such people think that life is one party. We drove by Recreio dos Bandeirantes until we reached a deserted beach. We got out. I left the headlights on.

We haven't done anything to you, he said.

You haven't? You've got to laugh. I felt the hate flooding through my ears, my hands, my mouth, all my body, a taste of vinegar and tears.

She's pregnant, he said pointing to the woman, it will be our first child.

I looked at the belly of the slim woman and decided to be merciful and said so, phut, above where I thought was her belly button, I disembodied the foetus immediately. The woman fell forward. I held the revolver to her temple and made a mine-sized hole there.

The man watched all this without saying a word, his wallet in the out-stretched hand. I took the wallet from his hand and threw it into the air and when it began to fall, I gave it a kick with my left foot, sending the wallet far away.

I tied his hands up behind his back with a rope I was carrying. I tied his feet afterwards.

Kneel down, I said.

He kneeled.

The headlamps of the car lit up his body. I knelt by his side, took off the bow-tie, folded the collar leaving his neck visible.

Lower your head, I ordered.

He lowered it. I lifted the machete up high, safely in two hands, I saw the stars in the sky, the vast night, the infinite firmament and brought down the machete, star of steel, with all my force, right in the middle of his neck.

The head did not fall and he tried to get up, uncertainly, like a dizzy hen in the hands of an incompetent cook. I gave him another swing and another and another and the head did not roll. He had fainted or had died with the bloody head attached to the neck. I put the body on the mudguard of the car. The neck was in a good position. I fixed my concentration like an athlete who is about to do a mortal dive. This time, whilst the machete was completing its short mutilating stroke, whistling and cutting the air, I knew that I would achieve what I wanted. Brock! the head went rolling onto the sand. I lifted the scimitar up high and recited: Hail the Collector! I gave a loud cry that wasn't any word, it was a long and strong howl, so that all creatures would tremble and get out of my way. Where I pass, the asphalt melts.

A black box under my arm. I say with a lisp that I am a plumber who is going to do some work for apartment two hundred and one. The hall porter finds my lisp funny and lets me go up. I start on the top floor. I am the plumber (speaking normally now) coming to do the work. Through the opening, two eyes: No, no one called for the plumber. I go down to the seventh, the same thing. I'm only going to be lucky on the first floor.

The maid opens the door for me and shouts inside, it's the plumber. A young woman in a night-dress appears, a bottle of nail varnish in her hand, pretty, about twenty-five years old.

There must be some mistake, she said, we don't need a plumber.

I took the Cobra out of the box. Yes, you do need one, you had better keep quiet or I'll kill the two of you. Is there anyone else at home? The husband was working and the little boy was at school. I tied up the maid, sealed her mouth with sticking plaster. I took the lady to the bedroom.

Take off your clothes.

I won't take off my clothes, she said, her head held high.

They owe me cough syrup, socks, cinema, filet mignon and pussy, hurry up. I gave her a punch in the head. She fell on the bed, a red mark on her face. Won't take them off! I tore off the night-dress, the panties. She wasn't wearing a bra. I opened up her legs. I placed my knees on her thighs. She had a lot of black pubic hair. She remained quiet, her eyes closed. To penetrate that dark forest wasn't easy, her pussy was tight and dry. I bent down, opened her vagina and spat inside, great gobs of spit. Even so it wasn't easy, I could feel my cock getting scratched. She moaned when I inserted my dick with all my strength to the end. Whilst I was inserting and withdrawing my cock, I licked her breasts, her ear, her neck, lightly running a finger over her arse, smoothing over her buttocks. My cock began to get lubricated with her vagina's juices, now warm and sticky.

As she no longer feared me, or because she did fear me, she came before I did. With the rest of the sperm that came from my cock I drew a circle around her navel.

Make sure that you don't open the door to a plumber again, I said, before going away.

I leave the attic in Visconde de Maguarape Street. A pan in each molar full of Dr Lustosa's wax/to chew with the front teeth/tossing off for a magazine photo/stolen books./I am going to the beach.

Two women are talking on the beach: one has her body tanned by the sun, a scarf on her head. The other is fair, she must go infrequently to the beach; both have very pretty bodies; the buttocks of the fair one are the prettiest buttocks I have ever seen. I sit nearby and keep watching them. They have noticed my interest and immediately begin to wriggle, communicating with their bodies, making provocative movements with their bums. At the beach we are all equals, we poor bastards and them. We are even better as we don't have that huge belly and those soft buttocks of the parasites. I want that white woman! She is also interested in me, she glances at me. They laugh and laugh, toothily. They say goodbye and the white one goes walking off in the direction of Ipanema, the water wetting her feet. I get near her and walk alongside, without knowing what to say.

I am a timid person, I have taken so many beatings in life, and her hair is fine and cared for, her chest is sleek, her breasts small, her thighs solid and rounded and muscular and the bum is made of two firm hemispheres. A ballerina's body.

Do you study ballet?

I have studied it, she says. She smiles at me. How can anybody have such a pretty mouth? I have the urge to lick every tooth in her mouth. Do you live near here? she asks. I do, I lie. She shows me a building facing the beach, all in marble.

Returning to Visconde de Maranguape Street. I while away the time to go to the house of the white woman. She's called Ana. I like Ana, a palindrome. I sharpen the large knife with a special stone, the neck of that dandy was very hard. The papers took up a lot of space on the death of the couple I had executed in Barra. The girl was the daughter of one of those bastards who get rich in Sergipe or Piauí, robbing the poor, and then come to Rio, and the sons of the flat-heads who no longer have any accent, paint their hair blonde and say that they are descendants of the Dutch.

The social columnists were concerned. The high society couple I had done away with had had a trip booked to Paris. There is no longer any security in the streets, said the headlines of one paper. You've got to laugh. I threw some underpants into the air and tried to cut them with the machete, as Saladin did (with a silk handkerchief) in the film.

They don't make scimitars like they used to any more/I am a hecatomb/It wasn't either God or the Devil/ who made me an avenger/It was I myself/I am the Penis Man/I am the Collector.

I go to the bedroom where Dona Clotilde had been lying for three years. Dona Clotilde is the owner of the attic flat.

Do you want me to sweep the sitting-room? I ask.

No, my boy, I would just like you to give me my trinevral injection before you go out.

I sterilise the syringe and prepare the injection. Dona Clotilde's buttocks are dry like an old and crumpled sheet of rice paper.

You fell from the sky, my son, God sent you, she said.

There is nothing wrong with Dona Clotilde, she could get up to go and buy things in the supermarket. The illness is in her mind. After three years lying down, she only gets up to go to the toilet, she cannot really have any strength.

One of these days I will shoot her in the back of her head.

When I satisfy my rage, I am possessed by a sensation of victory, of euphoria that gives me the urge to dance – I give short howls, grunts, inarticulate sounds, closer to music than to poetry and my feet slide about the floor, my body moves in a rhythm of twists and leaps, like a savage or a monkey.

Whoever wants to order me about can do so, but he will die. I very much want to kill one of those television personalities who show their fatherly image of a successful old rascal, a person whose blood is thickened by caviar and champagne. Eat caviar/your day will come./ They are owing me a young girl of twenty, full of teeth and perfume. The girl from the marble building? I enter and she is waiting for me, seated in the sitting-room, quiet, immobile, her hair very black, her face white, she looks like a photograph.

Let's go out, I say to her. She asks if I had come by car. I tell her that I haven't got a car. She has. We go down in the service lift and exit in the garage, we get into a Puma convertible.

After some time I ask if I can drive and we change places. Is Petropolis alright? I ask. We drive up the mountain without saying a word, with her looking at me. When we arrive in Petropolis she asks me to stop at a restaurant. I say that I haven't any money or appetite but she has both, she eats voraciously as if they would take away her plate at any moment. At the next table is a group of young people drinking and talking loudly, young executives driving up on Friday and drinking before meeting their ladies all dolled up to play whist or to gossip whilst nibbling cheeses and wines. I hate executives. She finishes eating. And now? Now let's go back, I say, and we go down the mountain, with me driving like a ray of light and her watching me. My life has

90

no meaning, I've already thought of killing myself, she says.
I stop in Visconde de Maranguape Street. Do you live here?
I get out without saying anything. She gets out after me: Will
I see you again? I go inside and whilst I am going up the
stairs, I hear the noise of the car driving away.

Top Executive Club. You deserve the best relaxation, carried
out with care and understanding. Our masseuses are tho-
rough. Elegance and Discretion.

I make a note of the address and go to the area, a house,
in Ipanema. I wait for him to come out, dressed in grey
clothes, waistcoat, black case, polished shoes, tinted hair. I
take a paper from my pocket, just like someone who is looking for an address and I follow the guy to his car. Those
bastards always lock the car, they know the world is full of
robbers, which they also are, only nobody catches them;
whilst he is opening the car I push the revolver into his belly.
Two men facing each other, talking do not draw attention.
Holding a revolver at his ribs is more frightening but this
should only be done in deserted areas.

Keep quiet or I'll fill your executive belly with lead.

He has a petulant and at the same time a common air of
the ambitious social climber from the country, awed by the
social column, a buyer, conservative voter, Catholic, church
activist, patriot, expense-account holder and opportunist, his
children studying at PUC, his wife involved with interior
decoration and partner in a boutique.

What have you been up to, boss, has the masseuse frigged
you or sucked your cock?

You're a man, you know what it's like and understand
these things, he said. The chat of an executive with a taxi
driver or a lift operator. From Botucatu to the Directorate, he
thinks he's already faced all situations of crisis.

I'm not any bloody man, I say smoothly, I'm the Collector.

I am the Collector! I shout.

He begins to turn the colour of his clothes. He thinks I'm
mad and he hasn't yet faced a madman in his damned air-
conditioned office.

Let's go to your home, I say.

I don't live here in Rio, I live in São Paulo, he says. He's lost his courage but not his astuteness. What about the car? I ask. Car, which car? This car, with the Rio number plate? I've got a wife and three children, he changes the subject of the conversation. What's that? An apology, a password, habeas-corpus, safe conduct? I tell him to stop the car. Phut, phut, phut, a shot for each child, in the chest. Then one for the wife, in the head, phut.

I'm going to play football on the seafront to forget the girl who lives in the marble building. Three whole hours, my legs all bruised from the kicks I got, the big toe on my right foot swollen, probably broken. I sit sweating at the side of the pitch, next to a Creole reading O Dia. The headline interests me, I ask for a loan of the paper, the guy says if you wants to read the paper why don't you buy one? I don't get annoyed, the Creole hasn't many teeth, two or three, twisted and black. I say, alright, We're not going to fight because of this. I buy two hot dogs and two cokes and give half to him and he gives me the paper. The headline says: Police look for the madman with a Magnum. I give the paper back to the Creole. He doesn't take it, laughs at me whilst he chews with the front teeth, or more precisely with the front gums that are as sharp as razors through so much use. News item in the paper: A group of socialites from the South Zone making grand preparations for the traditional Christmas Ball – the first day of Carnival. The ball begins on the twenty-fourth and finishes on New Year's Day; Ranch owners from Argentina, heirs from Germany, American artists, Japanese executives are coming, international parasites. Christmas has become a real party. Drink, revelry, orgies, debauchery.

The First Cry of Carnival. You've got to laugh. These guys are funny.

A madman jumped off the Rio-Niterói bridge and floated for twelve house before a lifeboat found him. He didn't even catch a cold.

A fire at an old people's home killed forty residents, their families celebrated.

I have just given a trinevral injection to Dona Clotilde when the bell rings. No one ever rings the bell to the attic flat. Dona Clotilde has no family. I look from the balcony. It's Palindromic Ana.

We chat in the street. Are you running away from me? she asks. More or less, I say. I go with her to the attic. Dona Clotilde, I've a girl with me here, can I take her to the bed-room? My boy, the house is yours, do what you want, I only want to see the girl.

We stand by the side of the bed. Dona Clotilde looks at Ana for a long time. Her eyes fill with tears. I used to pray every night, she sobbed, every night that you meet a girl like this. She raises up high her thin arms covered in fine hairs, with her hands together and says, oh my God, how I thank you!

We are in my bedroom, standing up, eyebrow to eyebrow, as in the poem and I take off her clothes and she takes off mine and her body is so lovely that I feel a catch in my throat, tears on my face, eyes smarting, my hands shake and now we are lying down, one on top of the other, intertwined, sighing, and move, and move without stopping, she cries, her mouth open, her teeth white like those of a young eleph-ant oh, oh, I love your obsession! she cries, water and salt and sperm flow from our bodies, without stopping.

Now, a long time after, we are lying down looking hypnot-ised at one another until night falls and our faces shine in the dark and the perfume of her body permeates through the walls of the bedroom.

Ana wakes before me and the light is switched on. Do you only have books of poetry? All these guns, what are they for? She takes the Magnum from the wardrobe, white flesh and black steel, points it at me. I sit on the bed.

Do you want to shoot? You can fire it, the old woman won't hear. A bit higher. With the tip of my finger I lift the barrel to the height of my forehead. It doesn't hurt here.

Have you already killed someone? Ana aims the gun at my forehead.

Yes.

Did it feel good?

It did.

How?

A relief.

Like the two of us in bed?

No, no, something else. The reverse of it.

I'm not afraid of you, Ana says.

Nor me of you. I love you.

We talk until daybreak. I feel a sort of fever. I make coffee for Dona Clotilde and take it to her in bed. I'm going out with Ana, I tell her. God heard my prayers, says the old woman between sips.

Today is the twenty-fourth of December, the day of the Christmas Ball or First Day of Carnival. Palindromic Ana left home and is living with me. My hate now is different. I've a mission. I always had a mission and didn't know it. Now I know. Ana helped me to see. I know that if every poor bastard did as I do the world would be better and fairer. Ana taught me to use explosives and I think that I am already prepared for this change of scale. Killing individuals is a mystical thing and I have freed myself from this. In the Christmas Ball we will conventionally kill those we can. It will be my last inconsequent, romantic gesture. We choose the disgusting shoppers in a South Zone supermarket to start the new phase. They will be killed by a bomb of high explosive power. Goodbye, my machete, goodbye my dagger, my rifle, my Cobra Colt, goodbye my Magnum, today will be the last day you are used. I kiss my machete. I will explode those people, I will acquire prestige, I will be not only the madman with the Magnum. I will also never go out again to Flamengo Park to look at the trees, the trunks, the root, the leaves, the shade, choosing the tree I would like to have, that I always wanted to have, on a piece of earth-beaten land. I saw them growing in the park and it made me happy when it rained and the earth got waterlogged, the leaves washed by the rain, the wind shaking the branches, whilst the cars of the cheats used to drive by at high speed without looking at either side. I don't waste my time with dreams, anymore.

The whole world will know who you are, who we are, says Ana.

News item: The Governor will be dressed as Father Christmas. News item: less festivities and more meditation, let's purify the soul. News item: There will be no shortage of beer. There will be no shortage of turkey. News item: The Christmas festivities will cause more victims of road accidents and of assaults this year than in previous ones. The police and hospitals prepare themselves for Christmas celebrations. The Cardinal on television: The spirit of Christmas has been distorted, its meaning isn't this one, this story of Father Christmas is an unfortunate invention. The Cardinal states that Father Christmas is a fictitious clown.

Christmas Eve is a good day for these people to pay what they owe, says Ana. I myself want to kill the Father Christmas at the Ball with the machete, I say.

I read to Ana what I have written, our Christmas manifesto for the newspapers. No more going out to kill at random, without a defined objective. I did not know what I wanted, did not look for a practical result, my hate was being wasted. I was right in my impulses, my mistake was in not knowing who was the enemy and why he was the enemy. Now I know, Ana taught me. My example must also be followed by others, many others, it's only in that way that we will change the world. That is the synthesis of our manifesto.

I pack the guns into a suitcase. Ana shoots as well as I do, it's only the machete she doesn't know how to handle, but this weapon is now obsolete. We say goodbye to Dona Clotilde. We put the suitcase in the car. We are going to the Christmas Ball. There will be no shortage of beer or turkeys. Or blood. A cycle of my life is closing and another one opens up.

# TO KILL A MAN

## Jack London

*Jack London, author of modern classics as diverse as* The Call of
the Wild *and* The Iron Heel, *was born in San Francisco in 1876.
He left school at thirteen to work in a cannery and later spent
periods as a seaman, a mill worker, a hobo and a Klondike gold
digger – experiences which converted him to socialism – before
becoming a writer.*

*Of London's prolific output, the sum total of what can properly
be considered crime fiction is some six short stories. Aside, that is,
from the extraordinary novel* The Assassination Bureau Ltd.
*which he was working on at the time of his suicide in 1916. (The
book has since been completed by Robert L. Fish).*

*'To Kill A Man' was originally published in 1913. As well as a
crime story, it is an allegory of the struggle between the classes.*

Though dim night-lights burned she moved familiarly
through the big rooms and wide halls, seeking vainly the
half-finished book of verse she had mislaid and only now
remembered. When she turned on the lights in the drawing-
room, she disclosed herself clad in a sweeping negligée gown
of soft rose-coloured stuff, throat and shoulders smothered
in lace. Her rings were still on her fingers, her massed yellow
hair had not yet been taken down. She was delicately, grace-
fully beautiful, with slender, oval face, red lips, a faint colour
in the cheeks, and blue eyes of the chameleon sort that at
will stare wide with the innocence of girlhood, go hard and
grey and brilliantly cold, or flame up in hot wilfulness and
mastery.

She turned the lights off and passed out and down the

hall toward the morning-room. At the entrance she paused and listened. From farther on had come, not a noise, but an impression of movement. She could have sworn she had not heard anything, yet something had been different. The atmosphere of night quietude had been disturbed. She wondered what servant could be prowling about. Not the butler, who was notorious for retiring early save on special occasion. Nor could it be her maid, whom she had permitted to go out that evening.

Passing on to the dining-room, she found the door closed. Why she opened it and went in, she did not know, except for the feeling that the disturbing factor, whatever it might be, was there. The room was in darkness, and she felt her way to the button and pressed. As the blaze of light flashed on, she stepped back and cried out. It was a mere 'Oh!' and it was not loud.

Facing her, alongside the button, flat against the wall, was a man. In his hand, pointed toward her, was a revolver. She noticed, even in the shock of seeing him, that the weapon was black and exceedingly long-barrelled. She knew it for what it was, a Colt. He was a big sized man, roughly clad, brown-eyed and swarthy with sunburn. He seemed very cool. There was no wobble to the revolver, and it was directed toward her stomach, not from an outstretched arm, but from the hip, against which the forearm rested.

'Oh,' she said. 'I beg your pardon. You startled me. What do you want?'

'I reckon I want to get out,' he answered, with a humorous twitch to the lips. 'I've kind of lost my way in this here shebang, and if you'll kindly show me the door I'll cause no trouble and sure vamoose.'

'But what are you doing here?' she demanded, her voice touched with the sharpness of one used to authority.

'Plain robbing, Miss, that's all. I came snoopin' around to see what I could gather up. I thought you wan't home, seein' as I saw you pull out with your old man in an auto. I reckon that must a ben your pa, and you're Miss Setliffe.'

Mrs. Setliffe saw his mistake, appreciated the naive compliment, and decided not to undeceive him.

'How do you know I am Miss Setliffe?' she asked.

'This is old Setliffe's house, ain't it?

She nodded.

'I didn't know he had a daughter, but I reckon you must be her. And now, if it ain't botherin' you too much, I'd sure be obliged if you'd show me the way out.'

'But why should I? You are a robber, a burglar.'

'If I wan't an ornery shorthorn at the business, I'd be accumulatin' them rings on your fingers instead of being polite,' he retorted. 'I come to make a raise outa old Setliffe, and not to be robbing women-folks. If you get outa the way, I reckon I can find my own way out.'

Mrs Setliffe was a keen woman and she felt that from such a man there was little to fear. That he was not a typical criminal, she was certain. From his speech she knew he was not of the cities, and she seemed to sense the wider, homelier air of large spaces.

'Suppose I screamed?' she queried curiously. 'Suppose I made an outcry for help? You couldn't shoot me? . . . a woman?'

She noted the fleeting bafflement in his brown eyes. He answered slowly and thoughtfully, as if working out a difficult problem.

'I reckon, then, I'd have to choke you and maul you some bad.'

'A woman?'

'I'd sure have to,' he answered, and she saw his mouth set grimly. 'You're only a soft woman, but you see, Miss, I can't afford to go to jail. No, Miss, I sure can't. There's a friend of mine waitin' for me out West. He's in a hole, and I've got to help him out.' The mouth shaped even more grimly. 'I guess I could choke you without hurting you much to speak of.'

Her eyes took on a baby stare of innocent incredulity as she watched him.

99

RED HANDED

'I never met a burglar before,' she assured him, 'and I can't begin to tell you how interested I am.'

'I'm not a burglar, Miss. Not a real one,' he hastened to add as she looked her amused unbelief. 'It looks like it, me being here in your house. But it's the first time I ever tackled such a job. I needed the money – bad. Besides, I kind of look on it like collecting what's coming to me.'

'I don't understand,' she smiled encouragingly. 'You come here to rob, and to rob is to take what is not yours.'

'Yes, and no, in this here particular case. But I reckon I'd better be going now.'

He started for the door of the dining-room, but she interposed, and a very beautiful obstacle she made of herself. His left hand went out as if to grip her, then hesitated. He was patently awed by her soft womanhood.

'There!' she cried triumphantly. 'I knew you wouldn't.'

The man was embarrassed.

'I ain't never manhandled a woman yet,' he explained, 'and it don't come easy. But I sure will, if you set to screaming.'

'Won't you stay a few minutes and talk?' she urged. 'I'm so interested. I should like to hear you explain how burglary is collecting what is coming to you.'

He looked at her admiringly.

'I always thought women-folks were scairt of robbers,' he confessed. 'But you don't seem none.'

She laughed gaily.

'There are robbers and robbers, you know. I am not afraid of you, because I am confident you are not the sort of creature that would harm a woman. Come, talk with me a while. Nobody will disturb us. I am all alone. My – my father caught the night train to New York. The servants are all asleep. I should like to give you something to eat – women always prepare midnight suppers for the burglars they catch, at least they do in the magazine stories. But I don't know where to find the food. Perhaps you will have something to drink?'

He hesitated, and did not reply; but she could see the admiration for her growing in his eyes.

100

'You're not afraid?' she queried. 'I won't poison you, I promise. I'll drink with you to show you it is all right.'

'You sure are a surprise package of all right,' he declared, for the first time lowering the weapon and letting it hang at his side. 'No one don't need to tell me ever again that women-folks in cities is afraid. You ain't much – just a little soft pretty thing. But you've sure got the spunk. And you're trustful on top of it. There ain't many women, or men either, who'd treat a man with a gun the way you're treating me.'

She smiled her pleasure in the compliment, and her face was very earnest as she said -

'That is because I like your appearance. You are too decent-looking a man to be a robber. You oughtn't to do such things. If you are in bad luck you should go to work. Come, put away that nasty revolver and let us talk it over. The thing for you to do is to work.'

'Not in this burg,' he commented bitterly. 'I've walked two inches off the bottom of my legs trying to find a job. Honest, I was a fine large man once . . . before I started looking for a job.'

The merry laughter with which she greeted his sally obviously pleased him, and she was quick to note and take advantage of it. She moved directly away from the door and toward the sideboard.

'Come, you must tell me all about it while I get that drink for you. What will it be? Whisky?'

'Yes, ma'am,' he said, as he followed her, though he still carried the big revolver at his side, and though he glanced reluctantly at the unguarded open door.

She filled a glass for him at the sideboard.

'I promised to drink with you,' she said hesitatingly. 'But I don't like whisky. I . . . I prefer sherry.'

She lifted the sherry bottle tentatively for his consent.

'Sure,' he answered, with a nod. 'Whisky's a man's drink. I never like to see women at it. Wine's more their stuff.'

She raised her glass to his, her eyes meltingly sympathetic.

'Here's to finding you a good position – '

But she broke off at sight of the expression of surprised

101

disgust on his face. The glass, barely touched, was removed from his wry lips.

'What is the matter?' she asked anxiously. 'Don't you like it? Have I made a mistake?'

'It's sure funny whisky. Tastes like it got burned and smoked in the making.'

'Oh! How silly of me! I gave you Scotch. Of course you are accustomed to rye. Let me change it.'

She was almost solicitously maternal, as she replaced the glass with another and sought and found the proper bottle.

'Better?' she asked.

'Yes, ma'am. No smoke in it. It's sure the real good stuff. I ain't had a drink in a week. Kind of slick, that; oily, you know; not made in a chemical factory.'

'You are a drinking man?'

It was half a question, half a challenge.

'No, ma'am, not to speak of. I *have* rared up and ripsnorted at spells, but most unfrequent. But there is times when a good stiff jolt lands on the right spot kerchunk, and this is sure one of them. And now, thanking you for your kindness, ma'am, I'll just be a pulling along.'

But Mrs Setliffe did not want to lose her burglar. She was too poised a woman to possess much romance, but there was a thrill about the present situation that delighted her. Besides, she knew there was no danger. The man, despite his jaw and the steady brown eyes, was eminently tractable. Also, farther back in her consciousness glimmered the thought of an audience of admiring friends. It was too bad not to have that audience.

'You haven't explained how burglary, in your case, is merely collecting what's your own,' she said. 'Come, sit down, and tell me about it – here at the table.'

She manoeuvred for her own seat, and placed him across the corner from her. His alertness had not deserted him, as she noted, and his eyes roved sharply about, returning always with smouldering admiration to hers, but never resting long. And she noted likewise that while she spoke he was intent on listening for other sounds than those of her voice. Nor had he relinquished the revolver, which lay at the corner of the table between them, the butt close to his right hand.

But he was in a new habitat which he did not know. This man from the West, cunning in woodcraft and plainscraft, with eyes and ears open, tense and suspicious, did not know that under the table, close to her foot, was the push-button of an electric bell. He had never heard nor dreamed of such a contrivance, and his keenness and wariness went for naught.

'It's like this, Miss,' he began, in response to her urging. 'Old Setliffe done me up in a little deal once. It was raw, but it worked. Anything will work full and legal when it's got a few hundred million behind it. I'm not squealin', and I ain't taking a slam at your pa. He don't know me from Adam, and I reckon he don't know he done me outa anything. He's too big, thinking and dealing in millions, to ever hear of a small potato like me. He's an operator. He's got all kinds of experts thinking and planning and working for him, some of them, I hear, getting more cash salary than the President of the United States. I'm only one of thousands that have been done up by your pa, that's all.

'You see, ma'am, I had a little hole in the ground – a dinky, hydraulic, one-horse outfit of a mine. And when the Setliffe crowd shook down Idaho, and reorganized the smelter trust, and roped in the rest of the landscape, and put through the big hydraulic scheme at Twin Pines, why I sure got squeezed. I never had a run for my money. I was scratched off the card before the first heat. And so, to-night, being broke and my friend needing me bad, I just dropped around to make a raise outa your pa. Seeing as I needed it, it kinda was coming to me.'

'Granting all that you say is so,' she said, 'nevertheless it does not make house-breaking any the less house-breaking. You couldn't make such a defence in a court of law.'

'I know that,' he confessed meekly. 'What's right ain't always legal. And that's why I am so uncomfortable a-settin' here and talking with you. Not that I ain't enjoying your company – I sure do enjoy it – but I just can't afford to be

103

caught. I know what they'd do to me in this here city. There was a young fellow that got fifty years only last week for holding a man up on the street for two dollars and eighty-five cents. I read about it in the paper. When times is hard and they ain't no work, men get desperate. And then the other men who've got something to be robbed of get desperate, too, and they just sure soak it to the other fellows. If I got caught, I reckon I wouldn't get a mite less than ten years. That's why I'm hankering to be on my way.'

'No; wait.' She lifted a detaining hand, at the same time removing her foot from the bell, which she had been pressing intermittently.

'You haven't told me your name yet.'

He hesitated.

'Call me Dave.'

'Then . . . Dave . . .' she laughed with pretty confusion. 'Something must be done for you. You are a young man, and you are just at the beginning of a bad start. If you begin by attempting to collect what you think is coming to you, later on you will be collecting what you are perfectly sure isn't coming to you. And you know what the end will be. Instead of this, we must find something honourable for you to do.'

'I need the money, and I need it now,' he replied doggedly. 'It's not for myself, but for that friend I told you about. He's in a peck of trouble, and he's got to get his lift now or not at all.'

'I can find you a position,' she said quickly. 'And – yes, the very thing! – I'll lend you the money you want to send to your friend. This you can pay back out of your salary.'

'About three hundred would do,' he said slowly. 'Three hundred would pull him through. I'd work my fingers off for a year for that, and my keep, and a few cents to buy Bull Durham with.'

'Ah! You smoke! I never thought of it.'

Her hand went out over the revolver toward his hand, as she pointed to the tell-tale yellow stain on his fingers. At the same time her eyes measured the nearness of her own hand

104

and of his to the weapon. She ached to grip it in one swift movement. She was sure she could do it, and yet she was not sure; and so it was that she refrained as she withdrew her hand.

'Won't you smoke?' she invited.

'I'm 'most dying to.'

'Then do so. I don't mind. I really like it – cigarettes, I mean.'

With his left hand he dipped into his side pocket, brought out a loose wheat-straw paper, and shifted it to his right hand close by the revolver. Again he dipped, transferring to the paper a pinch of brown, flaky tobacco. Then he proceeded, both hands just over the revolver, to roll the cigarette.

'From the way you hover close to that nasty weapon, you seem to be afraid of me,' she challenged.

'Not exactly afraid of you, ma'am, but, under the circumstances, just a mite timid.'

'But I've not been afraid of you.'

'You've got nothing to lose.'

'My life,' she retorted.

'That's right,' he acknowledged promptly. 'And you ain't been scairt of me. Mebbe I am over anxious.'

'I wouldn't cause you any harm.' Even as she spoke, her slipper felt for the bell and pressed it. At the same time her eyes were earnest with a plea of honesty. 'You are a judge of men. I know it. And of women. Surely, when I am trying to persuade you from a criminal life and to get you honest work to do . . . ?'

He was immediately contrite.

'I sure beg your pardon, ma'am,' he said. 'I reckon my nervousness ain't complimentary.'

As he spoke, he drew his right hand from the table, and after lighting the cigarette, dropped it by his side.

'Thank you for your confidence,' she breathed softly, resolutely keeping her eyes from measuring the distance to the revolver, and keeping her foot pressed firmly on the bell.

'About three hundred,' he began. 'I can telegraph it West to-night. And I'll agree to work a year for it and my keep.'

'You will earn more than that. I can promise seventy-five dollars a month at the least. Do you know horses?'

His face lighted up and his eyes sparkled.

'Then go to work for me – or for my father, rather, though I engage all the servants. I need a second coachman – '

'And wear a uniform?' he interrupted sharply, the sneer of the free-born West in his voice and on his lips.

She smiled tolerantly.

'Evidently that won't do. Let me think. Yes. Can you break and handle colts?'

He nodded.

'We have a stock farm, and there's room for just such a man as you. Will you take it?'

'Will I, ma'am?' His voice was rich with gratitude and enthusiasm. 'Show me to it. I'll dig right in to-morrow. And I can sure promise you one thing, ma'am. You'll never be sorry for lending Hughie Luke a hand in his trouble – '

'I thought you said to call you Dave,' she chided forgivingly.

'I did, ma'am. I did. And I sure beg your pardon. It was just plain bluff. My real name is Hughie Luke. And if you'll give me the address of that stock farm of yours, and the railroad fare, I'll head for it first thing in the morning.'

Throughout the conversation she had never relaxed her attempts on the bell. She had pressed it in every alarming way – three shorts and a long, two and a long, and five. She had tried long series of shorts, and, once, she had held the button down for a solid three minutes. And she had been divided between objurgation of the stupid, heavy-sleeping butler and doubt if the bell were in order.

'I am so glad,' she said; 'so glad that you are willing. There won't be much to arrange. But you will first have to trust me while I go upstairs for my purse.' She saw the doubt flicker momentarily in his eyes, and added hastily, 'But you see I am trusting you with the three hundred dollars.'

'I believe you, ma'am,' he came back gallantly. 'Though I just can't help this nervousness.'

'Shall I go and get it?'

But before she could receive consent, a slight muffled jar from the distance came to her ear. She knew it for the swing-door of the butler's pantry. But so slight was it – more a faint vibration than a sound – that she would not have heard had not her ears been keyed and listening for it. Yet the man had heard. He was startled in his composed way.

'What was that?' he demanded.

For answer, her left hand flashed out to the revolver and brought it back. She had had the start of him, and she needed it, for the next instant his hand leaped up from his side, clutching emptiness where the revolver had been.

'Sit down!' she commanded sharply, in a voice new to him. 'Don't move. Keep your hands on the table.'

She had taken a lesson from him. Instead of holding the heavy weapon extended, the butt of it and her forearm rested on the table, the muzzle pointed, not at his head, but his chest. And he, looking coolly and obeying her commands, knew there was no chance of the kick-up of the recoil pro-ducing a miss. Also, he saw that the revolver did not wobble, nor the hands shake, and he was thoroughly conversant with the size of hole the soft-nosed bullets could make. He had eyes, not for her, but for the hammer, which had risen under the pressure of her forefinger on the trigger.

'I reckon I'd best warn you that that there trigger-pull is filed dreadful fine. Don't press too hard, or I'll have a hole in me the size of a walnut.'

She slacked the hammer partly down.

'That's better,' he commented. 'You'd best put it down all the way. You see how easy it works. If you want to, a quick light pull will jiffy her up and back and make a pretty mess all over your nice floor.'

A door opened behind him, and he heard somebody enter the room. But he did not turn his head. He was looking at her, and he found it the face of another woman – hard, cold, pitiless, yet brilliant in its beauty. The eyes, too, were hard, though blazing with a cold light.

'Thomas,' she commanded, 'go to the telephone and call the police. Why were you so long in answering?'

'I came as soon as I heard the bell, madam,' was the answer.

The robber never took his eyes from hers, nor did she from his, but at mention of the bell she noticed that his eyes were puzzled for the moment.

'Beg your pardon,' said the butler from behind, 'but wouldn't it be better for me to get a weapon and arouse the servants?'

'No; ring for the police. I can hold this man. Go and do it – quickly.'

With the butler gone she concentrated her attention on the robber. 'When you are in prison', she said coldly, 'you will have time to meditate upon what a fool you have been, taking other persons' property and threatening women with revolvers. You will have time to learn your lesson thoroughly. Now tell the truth. You haven't any friend in trouble. All that you told me was lies.'

He did not reply. Though his eyes were upon her, they seemed blank. In truth, for the instant she was veiled to him, and what he saw was the wide sunwashed spaces of the West, where men and women were bigger than the rotten denizens, as he had encountered them, of the thrice rotten cities of the East.

'Go on. Why don't you speak? Why don't you lie some more? Why don't you beg to be let off?'

'I might,' he answered, licking his dry lips. 'I might ask to be let off if . . .'

'If what?' she demanded peremptorily, as he paused.

'I was trying to think of a word you reminded me of. As I was saying, I might if you was a decent woman.'

Her face paled.

'Be careful,' she warned.

'You don't dast kill me,' he sneered. 'The world's a pretty low down place to have a thing like you prowling around in it, but it ain't so plumb low down, I reckon, as to let you put a hole in me. You're sure bad, but the trouble with you is that you're weak in your badness. It ain't much to kill a man, but you ain't got it in you. There's where you lose out.'

'Be careful of what you say,' she repeated. 'Or else, I warn you, it will go hard with you. It can be seen to whether your sentence is light or heavy.'

'Something's the matter with God,' he remarked irrelevantly, 'to be letting you around loose. It's clean beyond me what He's up to, playing such-like tricks on poor humanity. Now if I was God – '

'Well, you are not,' she sneered.

'Will you kindly answer one question, ma'am?' the man said. 'That servant fellow said something about a bell. I watched you like a cat, and you sure rung no bell.'

'It was under the table, you poor fool. I pressed it with my foot.'

'Thank you, ma'am. I reckoned I'd seen your kind before, and now I sure know I have. I spoke to you true and trusting, and all the time you was lying like hell to me.'

She laughed mockingly.

'Go on. Say what you wish. It is very interesting.'

'You made eyes at me, looking soft and kind, playing up all the time the fact that you wore skirts instead of pants – and all the time with your foot on the bell under the table. Well, there's some consolation. I'd sooner be poor Hughie Luke, doing his ten years, than be in your skin. Ma'am, hell is full of women like you.'

There was silence for a space, in which the man, never taking his eyes from her, studying her, was making up his mind.

'Go one,' she urged. 'Say something.'

'Yes, ma'am, I'll say something. I'll sure say something. Do you know what I'm going to do? I'm going to get right up from this chair and walk out that door. I'd take the gun from you, only you might turn foolish and let it go off. You can have the gun. It's a good one. As I was saying, I am going right out that door. And you ain't going to pull that gun off either. It takes guts to shoot a man, and you sure ain't got them. Now get ready and see if you can pull that trigger. I ain't going to harm you. I'm going out that door, and I'm starting.'

Keeping his eyes fixed on her, he pushed back the chair and slowly stood erect. The hammer rose halfway. She watched it. So did he.

'Pull harder,' he advised. 'It ain't half up yet. Go on and pull it and kill a man. That's what I said, kill a man, spatter his brains out on the floor, or slap a hole into him the size of your fist. That's what killing a man means.'

The hammer lowered jerkily but gently. The man turned his back and walked slowly to the door. She swung the revolver around so that it bore on his back. Twice again the hammer came up halfway and was reluctantly eased down.

At the door the man turned for a moment before passing on. A sneer was on his lips. He spoke to her in a low voice, almost drawling, but in it was the quintessence of all loathing as he called her a name unspeakable and vile.

# IF I QUENCH THEE . . .

## William E. Chambers

*William E. Chambers (1943– ) lives in New York. He is a graduate of the writing course run by the Mystery Writers of America and has written several crime novels and short stories. He is also an active member of the Communication Workers of America.*

*'If I Quench Thee . . .' is set in Manhattan and is the tale of the visit of WASP Arthur Stern to visit his daughter Monica there. The unusual title comes from a line in Shakespeare's* Othello, Act V. *The story was first published in 1977.*

Arthur Stern looked past his denim-clad daughter at the apartment she had taken in one of Manhattan's ghettos. It was the first time he had seen it and he frowned critically. A rickety wicker settee served as a couch. The top of an ancient and probably unworkable combination TV-radio cabinet was used as a bar, and held two bottles of cheap rye. The lifelike poster of Communist rebel Che Guevara that decorated the otherwise plain wall behind the bar deepened the hue of Stern's pink complexion. Closing the door behind him, he handed her his coat and said, 'For God's sake, Monica, put on a bra. There's not much to that blouse you're wearing.'

Monica stood on her toes and kissed his cheek. 'Don't be so old-fashioned. If God wanted these things bound, I would have been born with a Playtex living – '

'Damn it! That isn't funny!'

'OK! OK!' Raising her hands like a holdup victim, Monica retreated backward through beaded curtains to her bedroom.

She shouted from inside, 'Hey, I'm glad you came to visit, Dad.'

'Thought I'd surprise you since you never visit me.'

'I was going to get in touch with you – '

'I'll bet.'

'I was. I've got a surprise of my own.'

'Nothing you might say or do would surprise me any more.'

Monica returned, mixed two highballs, and sat on the settee next to Stern. They clinked glasses. He said, 'Happy birthday.'

'Whoa. I'm not twenty-four until next week. Don't rush it.'

'I didn't know what to give you as a present, Monica, so I thought I'd find out what you needed and write a check.'

'Well, I don't really *need* anything – '

'Seems to me you could use everything.'

'Like what? I have my home, my job – '

'Some home.'

'The location's convenient for work.'

'Toiling for peanuts among a bunch of savages – '

'Daddy – please! I do social work because I have a conscience.'

'What kind of conscience prods a daughter to leave her own flesh and blood for a band of slum dwellers?'

'You don't need me. These people do.'

'Need you? Do you think your mother – God rest her soul – and I slaved to build that mink farm just for ourselves?'

When Monica failed to answer, Stern continued, 'We did it to get *you* away from the city – the slums – and the kind of people who dwell in them.'

'These *kind* of people are good people, Dad. All they need is some help – '

'Bull! All they need is to get off their butts and help themselves like I did.'

Monica gulped her drink, took a deep breath and said, 'You've always been strong, Dad. That's why you can't understand people who are weak.'

112

The shrill buzz of the doorbell interrupted them, and Monica looked a little uncomfortable. Stern said, 'Expecting company?'

'No. Not really.' She fumbled with the buttons on her blouse. 'It – well – it might be Tod Humbert.'

'Another social worker?'

'Much more than that.'

A second, more insistent buzz made Stern wince.

'Buzz him back, will you?'

The sound of a man coming up the stairs was followed by a vigorous tapping on the door. Monica opened it and said, 'Oh – hi, Tod – '

A tall, thin black man wearing a short leather jacket and blue jeans wrapped his arms around her waist, kissed her on both cheeks and said, 'You're looking bad, baby. Superbad!'

Monica gently withdrew from his embrace and turned sheepishly toward her father.

'Tod – I – I want you to meet Arthur Stern, my father.'

A bright smile flashed across the black man's face. He walked forward, hand extended and said, 'Mr Stern, this is a pleasure, sir.'

Ignoring Tod completely, Stern rose. 'Monica, my coat please.'

The girl looked pleadingly at him, then went wordlessly into the bedroom. Tod sat down on the settee and stared silently at his outstretched legs and crossed ankles. Stern wrote out a check and handed it to Monica when she returned with his coat.

'Fill in whatever you need.'

'May I borrow your pen?'

'Of course. Here.'

Monica blinked steadily as she filled out the check and handed it back to him. The amount read: *Nothing*.

The odor of rancid food that pervaded the hall disappeared as Stern stepped into the cold night air. He crumpled the rejected check in his fist, threw it into the gutter and ordered himself to be calm. However, his stomach churned and his

113

temples throbbed as he envisioned the black man with his daughter, the black man's arms around Monica . . .

Stern strode around the block, trying to decide what to do. He could disown Monica and wash his hands of all responsibility toward her. But the very thought made him shudder. He could go home and hope time would heal the wounds. But what if that failed? Finally, he decided he could return to her apartment, make apologies and an effort to tolerate Humbert, and start rebuilding their damaged relationship.

Choice number three was most logical, of course, so Stern swallowed his pride and marched back to his daughter's building. An elderly man who was leaving held the inner door open as Stern entered, making it unnecessary for him to ring the bell. A shaft of yellow light slanting from the recessed hall at the top of the stairs indicated a partially opened apartment door. The sound of familiar voices made him hesitate at the foot of the landing. He heard Tod Humbert say, 'Don't feel bad, honey. It's good to be snubbed occasionally. Humbles the ego.'

'Thanks for being so understanding, Tod.'

'You're extra-special. Marrying you will be the greatest thrill of my life.'

A sudden upsurge of blood pressure made Stern grip the bannister rail for support. He had visions of friends and business associates sporting lewd grins and knowing leers. Damn it! He could stand her seeing Humbert, but not this – not marriage, a black son-in-law.

Fists clenched, teeth gritting, he left the building again and ducked into the doorway of an abandoned house diagonally across the street. The burning hatred he was feeling now conjured up remembrances a quarter-century old. His mind filled with reflections of Korea, of another people different in skin color, an alien race that had threatened him and his fellow commandoes. A threat he had eliminated with bullets, piano wire, and bare hands.

Once again, after twenty-five years, he felt threatened. But this type of threat was different, wasn't it? New York wasn't

114

a jungle – or was it? You couldn't react here the way you could in Korea – or could you . . . ?

If the sight of Tod Humbert emerging several minutes later from Monica's hallway stimulated Stern's adrenal glands, he showed no sign of it. He remained still until the black man disappeared around the corner, then he followed. After walking a deserted block, he called out, 'Mr Humbert!' Tod Humbert glanced warily over his shoulder. 'It's me, Arthur Stern.'

Stern broke into a trot to catch up, then feigned breathlessness. He said, 'I hope you can forgive my rude behavior. Monica and I had angry words before you arrived and I let my emotions get the best of me. I was just returning to apologize when I happened to see you.'

The black man chuckled, extended his hand and said, 'We all have our faults, don't – '

He never finished his sentence. Stern gripped his outstretched hand, jerked him forward and kneed him in the groin. As Tod's legs buckled, he clawed wildly. Stern felt a burning sensation on one side of his face and heard cloth tear. Both men collapsed against a row of foul-smelling garbage cans lined up before a run-down tenement. The clatter of metal and the screech of an exasperated cat shattered the night. Stern crawled on top of Humbert, gripped his hair with both hands and pounded his head against the sidewalk. An edge-of-the-hand chop across the black man's throat ended the conflict.

Stern lumbered to his feet, glanced about, then twisted his tie and tore his shirt. The facial cut he had received before falling bled enough to satisfy him. He knew that muggings occurred with startling regularity in this section of New York City. He imagined how Monica would feel when her own father was victimized. It would be The Lesson that would teach her to despise the ghetto dwellers for the depths to which most of them sunk, and bring her home again to her own kind. Especially when his attacker was Tod Humbert!

Yellow squares of light began flashing in various tenements, and somewhere nearby a window rattled open. Stern clutched his wounded face with one hand and staggered into the gutter shouting for the police.

Arthur Stern gestured in disbelief as he spoke to the bored, flat-faced detective sitting across the desk from him. 'As I told the patrolmen, I was just walking along when this man attacked me. I came back to the neighborhood because I wanted to talk to my daughter again. You can imagine my shock – my – my horror when the mugger turned out to be the man my daughter had introduced me to only an hour earlier. The man – my God – the man she was going to marry – '

A detective put his head through the door. 'His daughter's here.'

'Send her in.'

Monica, complexion drained, entered listlessly. Stern went to her and gently squeezed her shoulders, saying, 'Thanks for coming, baby.'

She stood stiffly, not returning the embrace. Instead, she said coldly, 'I thought they handcuffed murderers.'

Stern felt a sudden chill on his back. He clutched her harder. 'It was self-defense,' he said. 'Humbert tried to mug me.'

'Tod could never raise his hand in violence to anyone. It would be against his principles, his way of life. If there was violence, *you* caused it. And I'll tell that to a jury. You murdered someone very dear to me.'

'It isn't murder when . . . someone like that . . .' Stern looked at the flat-faced detective, who was watching him closely. Then he shook his head, hissed air in through clenched teeth and said, 'Damn it! How could you even *think* of marrying him, Monica!'

'Marry him? What are you talking about?'

'Don't pretend! I came back to apologize tonight and overheard your conversation from the hall. He said marrying you would be the greatest thrill of his life.'

Monica stared at him for a long moment. Then she shrugged his hands from her shoulders, fumbled through

116

her purse and produced a snapshot of a blond man in an army medical uniform. 'This is the surprise I had for you, Dad. Next month I'm going to marry *this* man.'

Stern's eyes grew wide as they rested on the picture. He tried to speak but his voice failed him. For the first time in his life, Arthur Stern knew fear as Monica's tear-stained face moved from side to side and he heard her say, 'Tod was going to marry me, all right. He – he was an ordained minister . . .'

# THE FLAW IN THE SYSTEM

## Jim Thompson

*Jim Thompson (1906–1976) was a director of the Federal Writers'
Project in Oklahoma during the Depression. He later worked, among
other things, as a steeple-jack and professional gambler before his
career as a writer for mass paperback publishers like Lion took off
in the early 1950s. Thompson was not only one of the most talented
of the 'pulp' writers (something which is only now being recognised),
he was one of the most political and much of his fiction is concerned
with exposing the Nightmare behind the American Dream.*

*'The Flaw in the System' (1957) is one of Thompson's more quirky
pieces, but the social comment and message are absolutely typical of
him.*

I watched him as he came up the mezzanine steps to the
Credit Department, studying his worn suit, his frayed neck-
tie, his scuffed shoes. Knowing, even as I waved him to a
new-account booth – with the very first question I asked him
– that he was strictly on the sour side. And feeling a kind of
surly happiness in the knowledge.

For an instalment house – a-dollar-down-dollar-the-rest-of-
your-life outfit – we didn't catch many sour ones. They knew
they couldn't beat us – how can you fast-talk a machine? –
so they left us alone. But here was this guy, an n.g. from
the word go, with a hundred and seventy-five bucks in sales
slips! I wondered what the hell was wrong with our clerks,
why they hadn't sent him up for an okay in the beginning
instead of wasting their time on him.

I looked up from the slips, sharply, all set to read him off.
I looked into his eyes – the warmest, friendliest eyes I had

ever seen, in the kindliest face I had ever seen. And all I could think of was that somehow, in some way acceptable to the home office, I had to let him have the stuff. I spoke to him, asked him a question, in a tone that was almost pleading and apologetic. He shook his head.

'No,' he said pleasantly. 'I cannot make a 50 per cent down payment. The fact of the matter is, I cannot make any down payment at all.'

'Well,' I said regretfully, 'I'm awfully sorry, sir, but I don't think – '

I broke off, unable to tell him, however politely, that the deal was no soap. I had a feeling that if the friendly warmth in those eyes died out, something very necessary to me would die with it.

So I filled out a sales contract – just writing down the answers he gave me without comment or further discussion. When I was through, I made a few telephone calls and then I took the contract in to Dan Murrow's office. Dan was our credit manager.

He scanned the contract swiftly, and then headed outside. I stayed where I was, listening.

I heard Dan say, 'Now, look, Mister. I don't know what you're trying to pull, see, but – ' And then his voice changed. Suddenly it became the same way mine had been, soft and humble and apologetic. Begging for the good will of a man who was not only a total stranger, but an out-and-out deadbeat to boot.

Well . . .

The guy left. Dan came back into his office, gave me a thousand-watt glare, and jerked his thumb toward the door. He didn't say anything. It didn't look like a good time for me to say anything, so I went back to my desk and made out a duplicate on the contract.

All our records were made in duplicate, the dupes going to the home-office store and to Mr Dorrance, the head credit manager. Mr Dorrance trusted no one. He left nothing to chance. As long as you did exactly as you were instructed to do, you were all right. If you didn't – well, however sharp

120

and tough you were, Dorrance was a lot sharper and a lot tougher. He had his eye on you all the time, and he made sure you knew it.

It was a good system. You might get sore at the whole blasted world, or you might get to where you just didn't give a damn, or you might even quit. But the system rocked right along, permitting no errors, working perfectly.

At least, it always had worked perfectly until now.

Dan Murrow didn't speak to me for the rest of the afternoon. But by quitting time he had straightened out a little, and we went to a place for a few beers. He was still kind of on the belligerent side. Sheepishly belligerent. He knew the account was sour – that is just couldn't be anything else – but he tried to pretend it wasn't.

'A hundred and seventy-five bucks,' he said. 'With our mark-up, that's around ninety dollars profit. What kind of credit manager would I be if I chased away that kind of dough?'

'Yeah,' I said. 'I guess that's right.'

'So maybe he's a toughie,' Murrow went on. 'We got a legal department, ain't we? We've got collectors – boys that know how to make the tough ones soft. Sooner or later we'll catch that cookie on a job, and when we do . . .'

His voice trailed away. He looked at me, his eyes strangely bewildered.

Obviously we weren't going to catch the guy on a job. We weren't going to catch him with any attachable assets. This would be the way he made his living – by gypping stores and hocking or selling the merchandise.

It wasn't fraud, because there'd been no misrepresentation. He was a dead-beat but, legally speaking, he wasn't a crook.

His first payment fell due on the following Saturday. Naturally he didn't meet it, so Murrow put a collector onto him. The collector reported back that the guy had skipped town. Whether he was lying or not, I don't know. Murrow had an idea that he was, but he couldn't see that it mattered much.

'*If* we could collect,' he said, '*if* – which we can't – it wouldn't help us any with Dorrance. We broke the rules, see? Like drawing to an inside straight, only ten times worse. Maybe a miracle might happen, and we'd fill the straight. But it's still all wrong. We could pay this account ourselves but Dorrance wouldn't like it one jot better.'

We sweated out the week-end, wondering what Dorrance would do and knowing that whatever it was, it wouldn't be nice. Late Monday afternoon Murrow came to the door of his office and motioned for me to come inside. He looked a little pale. His hand shook as he closed the door behind me.

'Dorrance?' I said.

'Yeah. His secretary, I mean,' Murrow grinned sickishly, trying to make his voice sound satirical. 'Mr Dorrance wants a full report on that very peculiar account,' he recited. 'A detailed report, setting forth any reasons we have – *if* we have any – for opening such an account.'

'Yeah?' I said. 'Well . . .'

'We got to think of something, Joe.' He leaned across the desk, desperately. 'Some way we got to get ourselves off the hook. It means our jobs if we don't. It might mean even more than that. Yeah,' he nodded, as I looked at him startled. 'We had no good reason to okay that guy, so could be we had a bad one. But then again maybe we were in cahoots with him, splitting the take.'

'Well . . .' I spread my hands helplessly,.

'Let's start at the beginning,' Murrow said. 'Why did you do what you did, anyway? Why didn't you just turn this character down yourself instead of passing him onto me?'

'I – well, I just didn't want to,' I said. 'It wasn't as if he was compelling me, or hypnotising me, or anything like that. And it wasn't because I felt sorry for him. It was just – well, it doesn't make any sense – it sounds crazy now. But – but–'

'I know,' Murrow murmured. And then he brought him-self up sharp. 'Go on and spill it! Maybe we can come up with something.'

'Well,' I hesitated. 'It was like I had to do it to prove something. That I was a person – a human being, not just part of a system. That there wasn't any system big enough to keep me from making a mistake just like there wasn't any big enough to keep me from doing the right thing. So – well, I guess that's why I did it. Because it was the only way, it seemed, that this guy would go on liking me. And I was afraid that if he ever stopped liking me, I – I just wouldn't be any more. I'd have moved off into a world I could never come back from.'

Murrow looked at me silently. After a moment he let out a scornful grunt – rather, he tried to. 'Brother!' he snorted. 'Are you a big help!'

'How about you?' I said. 'Why didn't you give him a turn-down?'

'Never mind about me!' he snapped. 'Because I'm stupid, that's why. Because I got so many dumb clucks working for me, I'm getting dumb myself . . . Well, you got anything else to say?'

I shook my head. 'Nothing that would make any sense.'

'Let's have it,' Murrow said wearily. 'You haven't *been* making any sense, so why should you begin now?'

'I was just wondering,' I said. 'I mean, I wasn't wondering exactly, but – He stuck two other stores in town besides ours. He could have made a clean sweep, yet he only took two. But those two are the same kind of outfits we are.'

'So?' Murrow frowned. 'So he plays the instalment houses. What about it?'

'Not just instalment houses. A certain *type* of instalment house,' I said. 'The hardboiled kind. The iron-clad system houses. Places where every contingency is provided for by the system, where the human element is ruled out. . . . The system says no sales to the unemployed. No sales to transients. It says that if a risk looks very bad, we must insist on a down payment which practically covers the wholesale cost of the merchandise. It allows for *no* exceptions under *any* circumstances. It doesn't allow us to think or to feel – to do anything but apply our own special yardstick and throw out anyone who doesn't measure up to each and every one of the rules. Why, one of the saints themselves could walk in here and if he didn't – '

123

'Chop it off,' Murrow said. 'Get to the point.'

'I've already got to it,' I said. 'This guy knows exactly how we operate – yet he chooses us. He deliberately makes things tough on himself. Why did he do it? – if he was just after the merchandise. If, I mean, he was doing it just for himself instead of – uh – '

'Yeah?' Murrow said grimly. 'Yeah?'

'Nothing.' I turned toward the door. 'I guess I'd better be getting back to work.'

Naturally he didn't send any report to Dorrance – how could he? There was nothing to report. And there was nothing we could do but wait until Dorrance called again . . . demanding an explanation for the unexplainable.

But Dorrance didn't call.

A week passed.

Two weeks.

And there wasn't a single peep from the home store.

I suggested to Murrow hopefully that maybe there had been a slip-up, that the matter had got buried somewhere and was now in the process of being forgotten. But Murrow said there wasn't a chance – not with our system.

'That's what they want us to think – that we got away with something. We think that, see, so maybe we'll try something else. And when we do . . .'

'But we aren't going to! We haven't tried anything yet, have we? We made this one mistake – kind of a mistake – but from now on–'

'I'll tell you what,' Murrow said. 'If you've borrowed anything against your petty cash, you'd better pay it back. Check the collectors – make sure they don't hold dough over from one day to the next. Keep your accounts posted right up to the minute. Have everything in perfect order, understand? Because if it isn't – if there's anything wrong at all – we'll be in the soup. A hell of a lot deeper than we are right now.'

I did what he told me to.

Four days later Dorrance showed up. It was on a Saturday, a few minutes before closing time.

He answered our nervous greetings with the merest of

nods. He cleared off a desk – waving me away when I started to help him – and started laying out the contents of two heavy briefcases.

'All right,' he said, spreading out his records – picking one contract, *the* contract, from among them, and placing it deliberately to one side. 'You know why I'm here. If I want to know anything I'll ask you. If I want you to do anything I'll tell you. Got that? Good. Now open up the safe, unlock the cash drawer, and bring your account files over here.'

It was almost midnight when he finished checking us. Almost five hours – with Murrow and me hanging around red-faced and embarrassed. Feeling unaccountably guilty, and looking a hell of a lot guiltier.

Five solid hours of waiting and watching – while Dorrance did his damnedest to spot something crooked.

Then, at last, he was through. He leaned back in his chair, massaged his eyes briefly with a thumb and forefinger, and gave us another of those infinitesimal nods.

'That does it,' he said. 'You boys are okay.'

Something inside of me snapped. Before I could stop myself I blurted out an angry, 'Thanks. I'll bet that disappoints you, doesn't it?'

'Now, now,' Murrow said quickly. 'Mr Dorrance is just doing his job.'

'Then it's one hell of a job!' I said. 'He comes in here late at night and – '

'Yes,' said Dorrance quietly. 'Yes, it's one hell of a job, son. I'll be glad to see the day when it isn't necessary – which, unfortunately, it seems to be at present. This is the tenth store I've hit in the past three weeks. Four of them didn't check.'

'Well,' I said. 'I didn't mean to say that – that – '

'It gave me quite a start,' Dorrance went on. 'Of course, there's always bound to be a little gypping – one-shot, off-and-on stuff. But these birds have been doing it regularly. They'd invented a system for beating our system . . . I wonder' – he hesitated, then his eyes strayed to that laid-aside contract. 'I've been wondering why I didn't foresee

that it would happen. We've discouraged individuality, anything in the way of original thinking. All decisions were
made at the top, and passed down. Honesty, loyalty – we
didn't feel that we had to worry about those things. The
system would take care of them. The way the system worked
– supposedly – a man simply *had* to be loyal and honest.

'Well, obviously, we were all wet: we found those four
stores I mentioned, and God knows how many others there
are like them. And about all I can say is we were asking for
it. If you won't let a man think for you, he'll think against
you. If you don't have any feeling for *him*, you can't expect
him to have any for *you*.'

He paused, picked up that lone contract, and glanced at us
questioningly, Murrow and I didn't say anything. Dorrance
shrugged.

'Now let's face it,' he said. 'This man has stuck store after
store in our chain. He's hit us for thousands of dollars. How
he got away with it, we don't know. None of our men have
been able to explain. But there *is* an explanation – several of
'em, in fact . . . Perhaps he worked for an outfit like ours at
one time. He knew you people had been pushed to the top
of the arc in one direction, and that you were all set to swing
the other way – out of resentment, frustration, anger. The
desire to do something for once that *didn't* make any sense.
All he had to do was catch you at the right time, and you'd
let him walk off with the store.

'Or it could be that he's simply a damn clever con man
operating in a new field. A good con man would know that
the easiest people to take are those who've never been taken
– people who supposedly know all the angles, who are so
sure that no one would even try to beat them that they're a
cinch for the first man who does.

'He's a very dangerous man. He did us a good turn,
indirectly, by starting this investigation, but that doesn't
change the situation. He's a menace – as dangerous as they
come – and if we ever spot him again he's got to be treated
as one. Just grab him, understand? Latch onto him, and we'll
figure out a legal charge later. Why, a man like that – he

126

could wreck us if he took a notion to! He could wreck our entire economy!'

Murrow glanced uneasily at the contract, wondering, as I did, what Dorrance intended to do about it. And about us. Then Murrow said nervously that he didn't imagine the guy would be back. 'Do you, Mr. Dorrance?'

'Why not?' Dorrance snapped. 'Why don't you think he'll be back?'

'Well' – Murrow looked at me uncomfortably. 'I'm not sure, of course. It was just an idea. But – '

'Dan means that it wouldn't be smart for him to come back,' I said. 'He'd know that we'd be on the lookout for him.'

'Oh,' said Dorrance. After a long moment he pushed himself up from his chair and reached for his coat. 'That wraps it up, I guess. Now let's get out of here. You boys have to work tomorrow, and I have to travel. As for the contract, throw it in your p-and-l's. Can't collect on it, so it may as well go into profit-and-loss.'

Murrow and I didn't move; we just weren't up to moving yet. And we couldn't think of anything to say either. But there was an unspoken question in the air. Dorrance answered it snappishly, as he packed his briefcases.

'What's the matter with you?' he said, not looking at us. 'You can't put two and two together? Do I have to draw you a diagram? That fellow hit the home store too – hit us the hardest of all. I personally okayed him for four hundred dollars . . .'

He sounded sore, but he didn't look it. Somehow he looked happy.

# THE FIVE PIN STANDS ALONE

## Gordon DeMarco

*Gordon DeMarco (1944– ) attended graduate school at San Francisco State College, where he became a participant in the 1968–69 student strike and co-chairperson of Students for a Democratic Society (SDS). Since then he has worked as a dishwasher, a chauffeur, a docker, a worker in a puppet centre and a teacher. He is now a full-time writer and has written plays and books on politics and history. His previous crime fiction includes* The Canvas Prison, October Heat *and* Frisco Blues. *Like those books, the following novelette features private eye Riley Kovachs, and blends tough-guy style with left-wing politics.*

*'The Five Pin Stands Alone' is published here for the first time. It is set in San Francisco in the 1950s.*

I was in the eighth frame of my third game at the Paradise Lanes. I was already thinking about a couple wet ones I would get at the 11th Frame, the bowling alley's cocktail lounge, when I heard a woman scream.

Everybody in the joint looked over in the direction of the mixed league bowling on alleys ten through twenty. I dropped my hand towel and hurried over to see what the commotion was all about. A large group of people in white bowling shirts with different colored collars were huddled around the ball return on the 18th lane. I pushed my way through the crowd like a 16 pound ebony plowing into the 1–3 pocket.

I saw him lying there face down on the hardwood alley with a very permanent looking hole in his back. It was neatly placed between the two words of stitched lettering on his shirt which read 'Scaparelli Trucking'.

'He just bent over to get his ball,' said a man shaking his head. He had a 160 going into the 7th and was working off back-to-back strikes. Could've been the best game of his life if he had picked up that 9–10 spare.'

'Yeah,' I said, 'instead it turned out to be his last game. Hope it doesn't blow the team average.'

'Hey mister, don't get me wrong. Johnny and me were buddies. Been bowling in the same leagues since I don't know when. Yeah, me'n Johnny goes way back.'

'Real pals, you two. Only he didn't make that spare. I hope you can forgive him.'

'Hey, I don't need your lip, mister. This is a real shock to me. A real shock. I doubt if I will be able to finish my game.'

'Yeah, sometimes life can throw you a gutter ball.'

Most everybody had been cleared out when the cops and ambulance arrived. But they were still curious. Forty, maybe fifty people, all but a few from the Bay City Guys and Gals Industrial League, the league in which the dead man had bowled, were hanging over the waist-high wall above the sunken lanes staring silently at the cops, photographers and ambulance attendants who wrapped the body and hauled it away.

I stuck around trying to get the lowdown on the stiffing. Tongues loosened when I told them I was in the business. From a couple members of Scaparelli Trucking, I learned that the dead bowler was named Johnny Scaduto and that he was a driver for Scaparelli's. Seems he was very popular among San Francisco area truck drivers and was running for union president in an election that was less than a week away.

'Johnny was a shoe-in,' said Mabel Myers, a dispatcher at Scaparelli's and a 135 scratch bowler for the Blue Devils, as the Scaparelli team was called. 'He could've beat Ike, the guy was so popular. He was the leader of the TDA.'

I scratched my chin. 'Truckers for Democratic Action?'

'Yes, him and Biff Lasky. They had the crooks in our local on the run.'

'That's right, mister,' said a man wearing a bowling shirt with a red collar. 'Johnny stood up to Gus Lemmons and his blasters. He had more guts than a sausage factory. If they didn't put that bullet in Johnny's back then I'm a monkey's uncle.'

'Can you help us find Johnny's killer, mister?' asked Mabel Myers pleadingly.

'Now that all depends,' I said, taking a Chesterfield out of my shirt pocket. I tamped it a couple of times on my wrist watch to settle the tobacco.

'You mean money, mister?' Mabel Myers asked, like if I had been on the Titanic I would've been the guy selling tickets to the life boats.

'I don't want to sound like a French mercenary, but it's something I make a living at. Like the guys driving truck, I need to get paid. To keep the landlord from kicking in the door when I come up short at the beginning of the month and to fight the knight-on-the-white-horse complex I sometimes get.'

'The man's got a good point, Mabel,' said the man in the red collared shirt. 'A guy's gotta eat. No argument there. None at all. How much you charge, mister?'

'Normally, it's $30 a day plus expenses.' The three of them whistled with astonishment. 'But then this isn't normal, is it? A man getting killed in a bowling alley – my alley – a worker, a union militant. No, not normal at all. I'll get by on whatever you can come up with.'

A moment of financial soul searching among the three bowlers produced $50. 'There's more where that came from, mister. The TDA people will want to kick in. You can bet on that.'

I got a few names and phone numbers from them after showing them my license just in case they would have second thoughts in the morning about giving their dough to a stranger. I walked back to my alley and took my ball from the return and put it in my bag. I was untying my shoes when a cop, a certain Lt. Flange spotted me and walked over.

'Kovachs! You mixed up in this thing?' The Lt. demanded to know. We had crossed paths before.

'Lt.? Me? I'm a bowler. I'm on the way to my first 600 series when all the commotion starts. Cost me my concentration. My ball kept sliding out of the pocket. You know what I mean? I finished with a lousy 560. I figure I was gypped.'

'Still the same smart mouth, eh Kovachs?'

'I told you, Lt., I'm a bowler, a serious bowler.'

'And my grandmother lifts weights. Kovachs, this is a police matter and if you so much as stick your pinky in where it don't belong, I'll come down on you so hard you'll have to reach up to tie your shoes. You get my drift?'

'You know, Flange, sometimes you're just too much. You forget that I don't wet my pants when you lean on me. You've just got to remember to save that stuff for the jay-walkers and double-parkers. It's such a shame to waste all that creativity.'

Flange hitched up his pants and shot a pointed finger toward my chest like a toy arrow from a plastic bow. 'Shut up, Kovachs! You've been warned. That's all I have to say to you. Another word and I'm taking you downtown.' His face was as flushed as a porcelain toilet.

'What's the charge, Flange? Bowling out of season? Failing to pick up the 1–5–10 split?' I chuckled and walked away.

I heard Flange yelling at the back of my head. 'You've been warned, Kovachs! You've been warned!'

2

I left the Paradise Lanes to look up Biff Lasky, Johnny Scaduto's partner in the TDA. Lasky lived on the east side of

Bernal Heights. That is the area of the hill that has open fields and some of the streets are unpaved. The houses are in a cozy state of disrepair and the hillsides are stocked with fennel, wild radish, mustard and carrot. Reminds me a lot of small-town Appalachia.

Biff Lasky was a fireplug with a pair of fists that could pound nails through hard wood. In his mid forties, he was a union militant from the old school. He told me he had been one of the iron men who pushed a wooden rig back in the early thirties when the union was just getting off the ground.

'I was there in '34. In Minneapolis during the big Teamo strike. I used to drive with Farrel Dobbs and the Dunne brothers. Now there were some good unionists. Communists too. Belonged to Trotsky's party. I never joined 'em – the Trotskys – but they made a whole lot of sense when it come to running a union. I'd trust them before Dan Tobin any day of the week. Any goddamn day of the week.'

Biff Lasky was talking non-stop. He told me he had heard of Johnny Scaduto's murder only minutes before I got to his house. Talking seemed to be his way of dealing with his feelings.

'Yeah, Johnny and me and a few of the boys put together the TDA about three years ago. We had to. The mob and the pie cards were taking over. We had to stop them. A lot of people were getting hurt. You know what I'm talking about? Hijacked rigs, sabotage, brothers getting beat into soft cheese for standing up to sell-outs and refusing to haul hot cargo. Things like that.'

Biff Lasky reached into the pocket of his plain cotton shirt and pulled out a pack of Camels. He put one in his mouth and lit it with a book match. He looked out of the window of his living room as he talked to me, occasionally spitting bits of loose tobacco from his lips.

'Yeah, we took our lumps, too. Johnny an' me and some of the other boys. Lemmons's got a good collection of goons. Some of 'em are bikers who ride those big Harley-Davidsons. Punks! They're all punks. Every goddamn one of 'em.'

Biff Lasky paused for a minute. Then he looked down at

his enormous hands and closed them into fists. The muscles around his jaw drew tight. The next thing I knew there was a loud crash and the secondhand end table that stood next to the stuffed chair Biff Lasky was sitting in was a pile of tooth picks. I jumped about ten feet.

'Those lousy bums,' he shouted. 'Those goddamn lousy bums! They're going to pay for this! I'll take 'em out myself!'

Biff Lasky went to a closet located across the room and returned with a metal pipe about 18 inches long. He rapped it once across his open palm and then stuck it in his pants.

'You'll excuse me, pal, I've got some business down at the hall.' He pushed by me on his way to the door.

'Biff, if you do that, the TDA is dead!'

'Yeah, we're all dead men, but I'm going to make those thugs work for their dinner.'

I ran to the door in front of him. 'Look, man, don't lose your head.'

'Outta my way!' Biff Lasky shoved me aside like I was a cobweb. He yanked open the door and stepped outside.

'What's more important, Biff?' I called after him. 'Your personal feeling or the future of the TDA and the union? Some people have got a lot riding on you. If you go down to the hall now you will be letting them down. Selling them out! That's what you'll be doing, Lasky, selling them out!'

When those words reached his ears he spun around and began to charge me. Scenes from my boyhood in Ohio rushed by my consciousness. I had barely time to go into a crouch to lessen the impending destruction from 200 pounds of anger.

He stopped just in front of me, pulled the lead pipe from his pants and crashed it into the corner of the flower box that hung under the window next to the front door. The box snapped off like a thin pencil. Half-dead geraniums flew in every direction.

Biff Lasky sat down on the door step and buried his head in his hands. 'Johnny and me were in Minneapolis together,' he said in a shaky voice. 'He saved me from a beating by the cops at the Battle of Deputies Run. We were pals from that day on. Comrades in struggle. A coupla musketeers.'

'Yeah, it's got to be tough to lose somebody like Johnny Scaduto. He must have been something.'

'He was an ace. A goddamn ace of spades. But you're right. Bustin' heads won't bring the man back, though I can tell you it would make me feel a hell of a lot better than I do now.'

'Yeah, revenge is the sweetest balm there is.'

'What?'

'Just something I read somewhere. Come on Biff, how 'bout I make us some coffee.'

Biff Lasky nodded. He got up from the step and we went back inside to talk about an alternative to a war of chains and pipes with the bully boys who worked for the Lemmons' regime.

3

Following two cups each of diesel-strength coffee, I agreed to let Biff Lasky go down to Scaparelli Trucking with me to ask some questions. I would have preferred to go alone, in fact would have insisted on it, but I had the good sense to know that one didn't insist with Biff Lasky.

Scaparelli's was a medium-sized outfit down on the Bay-shore near the Daly City line. It was night, but the dock was lit up with overhead floodlights. Several mechanics were working on a couple of middle-aged cabs. A small knot of drivers were huddled together on the loading dock. Biff Lasky knew two of the drivers, fellows named Mickey Mee-cham and Butch Hegan. Both were supporters of the rebel truckers' movement but, according to Lasky, they were not frontline activists.

'Mickey!' hailed Biff Lasky from twenty yards away. The whole yard turned towards us. So much for doing things on the "qt". 'Hey Mickey!' Lasky hollered once again. 'Hey, all you guys! Come here!'

The mechanics and truckers in the yard moved briskly to where Biff Lasky had planted himself.

'I guess you guys heard about brother Scaduto by now,' Lasky said. Everyone dropped their heads in silent acknowledgement. 'Well, he was murdered! And if you don't know why, I'm here to tell you. Brother Scaduto was gunned down by Lemmons' goons because the TDA was going to expose his rotten corrupt regime. His years of sweetheart deals with Scaparelli and Creel and the other trucking bosses are numbered. They all knew we were going to win the election and throw them off the gravy train. Some of 'em knew they'd bounce all the way to the joint. I'm talking federal penitentiary.

'I'm here to tell you that even murder can't scare us off. They count on you being afraid that if you speak up they'll get you fired or break your legs, or if that don't work, put a goddamn slug in your back like they did to brother Scaduto. Johnny died for you an' me. You gotta remember that. You gotta remember the history of the labor movement is written in the blood of men an' women who stood up to the bosses and their stooges. We come a long way, brothers. And we can't give up now. If the TDA slate wins the election, the first thing we'll do is deliver Johnny Scaduto's killers. You can bet your bottom dollar on that.'

The men listened intently to Biff Lasky. Most expressed agreement with him. Not verbally, but you could tell by the look in their eyes.

Then the man called Mickey spoke. 'Biff, what can we do about Johnny's murder? I'm no fink, but if the union is involved some way, I say we call in the cops.'

'The hell with the cops!' Lasky fumed. 'This is an internal matter. We don't bring the cops in. We clean our own house.'

'But we don't have the kind of muscle the cops have,' protested another man.

'The hell, you say,' barked Lasky. 'We got all the muscle we need. The election's in a few days. That'll match any pipes and brass-knuckle goons Lemmons can throw at us.'

'Yeah, but what if the election is rigged?' said the same man. 'It wouldn't be the first time, you know.'

Biff paused, then said, 'Then it'll be war. It'll be open season.' He pounded a massive fist into an open hand.

'Hey, Lasky,' said a driver in a denim jacket. 'How come you're so sure the local's behind Scaduto's killing? Sounds like a cheap election trick to me.'

Without a word, Biff lunged at the man and had him by the throat before any of the small group of men could react and pull him off. It wasn't easy.

'Lemme at 'im!' He screamed, 'Lousy, goddamn Lemmons stooge. I'll pulverise 'im.'

The attacked driver, pulled free from Biff Lasky's vice-grip hands, rubbed his neck. 'That's why you and your pink pals will never get elected, Lasky,' he said. 'You do the bosses' dirty work always attacking the union. This goon squad stuff is just smoke. Scaduto got what was coming to him.'

'You lousy sonofabitch!' yelled Biff, being held in restraint by two men on each arm. 'You scab! You sell out! You're on my list, Packer!'

The impromptu rally and accompanying brawl brought Scaparelli's security force on the run. They told Lasky to vamoose before they cuffed him off to the clink. He spit a few oaths at the company bulls who had drawn their billy clubs before slowly and reluctantly retreating towards the car. I tagged along behind him.

As I was walking toward the parking lot, I felt a finger tap my shoulder. I turned to answer it.

'Hey, mister,' said the man Biff had pointed out as Butch Hegan. 'Are you with Biff?' I told him that, much to my chagrin, I was. 'Who are you, mister?' he asked. 'I've never seen you before, have I?'

'I was at the bowling alley when Johnny Scaduto got it.

137

Some people there wanted me to look into it. I'm a private investigator.'

The eyebrows on the man jumped up and touched the brim of his cap. 'A peeper?'

'Yeah, that, too,' I said.

'Who you working for?'

'Just some people.'

'Mabel Myers, I bet. She's Scaduto's sweetheart. Or at least she used to be until a couple months ago.'

'You got something to say, or are we just going to stand here and gossip?'

'Hey, I'm just asking. Johnny was a pal. We drove the day shift together for the last two years. Until a month ago when I was switched to nights. Hell, we're all pretty broken up over this.'

'Yeah, he was a popular guy. But like they say, it only takes one enemy.'

'Johnny had a lot of enemies, mister. I was going to tell Biff, but since you're the peeper, maybe I should tell you instead.'

'Tell me what?'

'I know how Biff feels about Johnny and the crooks running our local, but I think he's all wet to think Lemmons' crowd did him in.'

'Not their style?'

'No, nothing like that. They are capable of a lot of things, including murder.'

'Well, who then?'

'You can bet Jack Creel had something to do with it.'

'Okay. So who's Jack Creel?'

'He's the freight office manager for Scaparelli. He's been on the take for years. Short-weighting freight, doctoring invoices, making phony deliveries, trucking hot cargo. He specialises in athletic equipment, but you name it and if it's shady, Creel's got his mitts in it. The way I figure it, Johnny caught up with him. You know, had something on his operation. At least, that's the rumor around here. Well, I heard him talking with Creel couple weeks ago. I happened to be walking past Creel's office when I heard the two of them going at it.'

'Hey Kovachs!' Biff yelled loudly. 'You comin' or what?'

'Look,' I said to Hegan. 'I've got to get him home and cooled off. He's taking this real hard.'

'Biff takes everything hard.'

'So I've noticed.'

'But I guess that's why I like the guy. He's a fighter for the drivers. Always has been. Never got the credit Johnny did, but Biff Lasky won't take a back seat to anybody when it comes time to set up the working man's Hall of Fame.'

'Maybe you should come with us. Tell Biff what you know. Might help cool him off.'

'No, mister, not me. The feelings between Biff and me aren't exactly mutual. He doesn't trust college boys. You know what I mean?'

I said I did, but I didn't really. 'Let me call you tomorrow,' I said.

Hegan scribbled his phone number on a piece of paper. 'You can reach me here. Call after two. I sleep until then.'

He turned and walked back toward the loading dock. The honking of a car horn told me Biff Lasky had run out of what little patience he had left. I returned to my car and drove him home. On the way, he promised me two things. To stay away from the union hall and to let me work on the Scaduto killing on my own. It was progress.

4

I met with Butch Hegan the next afternoon at the Chat'N'Chew on Mission Street at Twenty-Fifth. Over cups of coffee a pint of homogenised cream couldn't have helped, he told me about the operation Creel ran.

'You see, Kovachs, a lot of shippers make small fortunes on the side. It's all in the way you write out your invoices and your ability to get a couple drivers you can rely on to pick up and deliver. It doesn't much matter if the cargo is cold or hot. Of course, there's more profit in hot cargo. All the drivers know what Creel is up to and know that Packer and a couple other drivers are making illegal runs. Like I told you, Creel specialises in stolen athletic equipment.'

'So, if everybody knows about it,' I said, asking the $64 question, 'how come Creel and Packer are getting away with it?'

'It's the way things are structured. Anybody pipes up, he gets fired by Creel or shoved around by Packer's boys. It's the same at other trucking companies. There was a driver a while back who started to raise a stink. He ended up sailing off the Coast Highway down near Pacifica. Police report said it was an accident, but everybody knows someone monkeyed with his rig.'

'Sounds like the rackets and the trucking bosses have a lock on this thing,' I said, shaking my head.

'That's just what it is. There's some feds snooping around the union. You know, investigating mob activities. Word is a secret Congressional Committee has been set up. I don't trust the government when it comes to union activities, but I'm like the rest of the guys. I'm not going to help them, but I'm not going to stand in their way, either.'

'What about the TDA and the election. Isn't that bound to change things if Lasky's group wins?'

'Don't get me wrong, Kovachs. I'm TDA all the way. I hope we win, even if the Communist Party is backing us. But I don't think that's going to change things all that much. A handful of militants are no match for the mob. Look what they did to Johnny Scaduto. Still it would be a beginning.'

'Let's get back to Johnny Scaduto. You told me last night about a rhubarb between him and Creel.'

'Two weeks ago. Maybe more. I was just clocking in. I had

to stop by payroll and straighten out a mistake in my last check. I passed Creel's office and heard him and Johnny going at it.'

Hegan lit his third cigarette as he began filling me in on the row between Creel and Scaduto. He said Creel threatened the teamster to keep his mouth shut if he didn't want any trouble. Scaduto told him to set fire to his pants.

'Then Creel said something that didn't make any sense to me,' said Hegan, swallowing the last mug of lukewarm coffee. 'Creel told Johnny to back off and clam up or the whole deal was off. And if he didn't, he said, he'd take Johnny down with him if there was any trouble.'

'What deal was he talking about?' I asked.

'Beats me. But those were Creel's words just like he said them. "If you don't clam up the whole deal is off".'

'Are you telling me that Johnny Scaduto was mixed up in Creel's hot cargo operation?'

'I don't know. I don't think so. I mean everybody knew Johnny was a pure union militant. Sympathetic to the Communists even. He goes back to Minneapolis, you know. The big strike. Hell, nobody would accuse Johnny of anything that wasn't on the up and up. Not even Biff.'

'Biff?' I said with a start. 'I thought Biff and Johnny Scaduto were the double play combination of the truckers' opposition.'

Hegan hesitated. 'Well, they are. Or were. I mean . . . Look, I've shot off my mouth too much already. I don't know you. For all I know, you might be with Lemmons' outfit.' He got up to leave.

'Whoa, slow down, willya?' I said, reaching over the table and putting my hand on his shoulder. 'If there was something between Scaduto and Lasky, I should know about it. You know how difficult it is to talk to Biff.'

'Yeah, you don't have to tell me that. But that's your problem. I'm not going to be the one to knock Biff or the TDA. Especially at this time. Besides, Kovachs, it was nothing, really. Nothing at all. Just one of Biff's temper

141

flareups. You know what I'm talking about. You talk to Creel if you want to find Scaduto's killer.'

Hegan rose from his seat and tossed a quarter on the table. 'I've got to be going. I'd say keep in touch, but I think I'd better button my lip until I find out about you.' He walked outside and disappeared in the Mission Street foot traffic.

5

I took Hegan's advice and went to Scaparelli's to talk to Creel. He had a small office cluttered with boxes and files of old invoices. Girly pictures hung on the wall above old, out of date calendars. Creel was on the phone when I entered.

'I don't care what kind of noises are coming from your gear box,' he barked into the mouthpiece. 'You get your ass to Stockton in the next hour or the only noise you'll be hearing is yourself being fired.' Creel looked up at me. 'Yeah? What do you want?'

'The name's Kovachs,' I said. The phone rang again. Creel picked it up.

'Yeah!' he said loudly. 'You're where? You dumb sonofabitch, you're supposed to be in Reno . . . I don't care who's sick . . . Tell it to the restaurants who're waiting for that vegetable shipment . . . You're on suspension Mallory! . . . For as long as I say, that's how long.' Creel slammed down the phone and looked up at me. 'The lousy sonofabitch missed his run and wants me to kiss his head and tell him it's okay. Some of these drivers just don't want to work. You know what I mean? They bellyache when their paycheck's a penny short, but when it comes to an honest day's work, they'd rather stay home and screw the old lady and get both their pay and my blessing for doing it. Who'd you say you were? What do you want?'

'Name's Kovachs. I'm what you might call a freelance wholesaler.' I winked, but Creel just stared at me without changing his expression. I went on. 'I got a great big overload of Ben Hogan autograph clubs. Woods, irons, putters, full sets. Got shoes and leather bags, too. Got ten dozen Brunswick bowling balls and bags. I can give the right guy a real good price.'

Creel took three inches of dead cigar out of a large glass ashtray next to the phone and lit it up. It took a moment to get it going. He leaned back in his big swivel chair. Something like a smile crossed his face.

'Now ain't that nice,' he said. 'A guy comes in off the street and wants to sell me a load of hot cargo for a "real good price." I suppose you want me to give you my personal check with my address and phone number on it.'

'Cash on the barrelhead, mate. No books, no looks.'

Creel jammed the butt of his cigar into the ashtray. He looked mad, but then that's the kind of guy he probably was. 'Just who the hell do you think you are, pal? I ought to call the cops right now. Trying to pass me hot stash. Get out of here before I lose my temper.'

'Sorry, mac. A pal told me you'd be interested. My mistake.' I turned and headed toward the door.

'What pal? Who told you to see me?' Creel was curious.

I turned my head back toward him without turning around. 'Skip it,' I said. 'Just wait'll I get my hands on Scaduto. I'll teach him to give me a wrong number.' I put my hand on the door knob and turned it.

'Johnny Scaduto?' Creel asked. A grownup dose of astonishment diluted his angry voice.

'How many Scaduto's you know?' I opened the door.

'Hey, why didn't you say so, mister?' Creel got up from his chair and started toward me. I walked out the door. 'Hey, come back here,' he called after me. 'I didn't know. Hey, let's talk about it.'

I kept going, hurrying through the loading dock until I

143

was out of sight. I could still hear Creel pleading with me to return.

<br>

## 6

Nobody ever said the labor movement was as pure as Rocky Mountain snow. It has had its share of crooks, opportunists, spies, sellouts, turncoats and organised gangsters. But each time one pops up it's a tough pill to swallow. It not only gives labor's reputation a shiner, but plants a straight hard one in the labanza of John and Jane Doe Rank-and-File. And to have a rank-and-file tough guy, an 'honest militant' as they say, get caught with his hand in the till. It's worse than finding out your sister makes a living entertaining the fleet. It gets you right in the guts. That's the way I felt pushing my Henry J up the Bayshore toward the Mission district.

But, hell, what did I really know? Maybe it was all smoke. The only thing implying Johnny Scaduto was a wormy apple was a twisted tale from Hegan and Creel setting his collar on fire when I mentioned Scaduto's name. Maybe it was nothing, but it was enough to take to Biff Lasky. I was interested to hear what he would have to say about it. I hoped we wouldn't have to go through him pulling his furniture apart again. Or me either, for that matter.

7

I decided it was in my interest to meet Lasky on neutral turf. Someplace away from his house. I called him from Beppo's Cafe on San Bruno Avenue and told him to meet me there in thirty minutes. He could have made it in ten, but I wanted to get a cappuccino under my belt before dealing with him.

I spent some minutes talking with Beppo. We were having an intelligent conversation about Cannelloni when Biff came through the door. 'Kovachs!' he said from the doorway. 'You better have something good!'

I motioned him to one of the small, round tables, the one farthest from Beppo and the two paying customers standing at the bar.

'Can I get you something to drink, Biff?' I asked as we sat down.

'You can get me Johnny's killer. That's what you can get me. Where've you been all day? I've been sitting around my house like a big dumbell waiting for you to call.'

'These things take time, Biff.'

'Time! We ain't got time!'

'I did get some info about Johnny Scaduto. It's pretty strange stuff and I don't know what to do with it. I'm going to need your help to make sense out of it.'

'What did you get?' Biff pulled a Camel from his coat pocket and lit it.

'What do you know about Creel, Biff?'

'Creel?'

'The freight boss at Scaparelli.'

'I know who he is! What does this have to do with Johnny?'

'I don't know, but your man Hegan told me Creel was trafficking in stolen sports gear, which I'm sure you know.

He also told me that Creel and Scaduto were having a giant
rhubarb in Creel's office about two weeks ago.'

'So?'

'So, Hegan overheard Creel telling Johnny if he didn't back
off, the whole deal was off.'

'Kovachs, you're not making sense. What deal?'

'That's what I'd like to know.'

'Hegan told you that?'

'Yes.'

'That bastard! I don't trust him. He's not a real trucker,
you know. Some kind of college boy playing at being a
teamo. A real shifty sonofabitch, if you know what I mean.'

'Maybe. But I saw Creel this afternoon and told him I was
a guy who had a warehouse full of hot bowling balls. He
was for throwing me out of his office until I told him I was
referred to him by Scaduto. He changed his tune quicker
than a bad harmonica player. I think he would have made a
deal with me on the spot if I had let him.'

Biff Lasky didn't say a word for about twenty seconds. His
eyes cut into mine like drill bits boring through soft bedrock.
Then, with a meaty fist, he pounded the table. The foam on
my cappuccino went flat.

'Kovachs, are you trying to tell me Johnny was teamed up
with Creel?' he said finally in a voice that sounded like Moses
indicting the Israelites.

I tried to qualify what I had said. 'I'm not trying to tell you
anything, Biff. I want you to tell me. What does it mean?'

'Bullshit! That's what it means. Kovachs, I thought you
were on our side. I'm not going to sit here and take this crap
from you or anyone.'

Biff rose from his chair and rolled his powerful shoulders.
But instead of pounding me into pudding, Biff pivoted on
his heels and stomped out of Beppo's. I caught up with him
at the door, but it was a half a block before I was able to
wrestle his attention to the ground and get him to stop.

'Look, Biff,' I said, 'don't you think it's time you stopped
blowing your top like a cheap tea kettle. It's the only way
we will ever be able to get to the bottom of this.'

He looked straight into my eyes for a long moment. Then he turned away and spoke into the traffic. 'I feel like knocking your block off, Kovachs, for what you said. But I know you ain't the enemy. It's this temper of mine. I guess it grew up ugly during all those years we had to fight the goddamn trucking bosses and their goons. A man had to have a short fuse and an iron jaw to survive those times. Otherwise, they'd tap dance on your face. I guess I just never learned when to shut it off.'

'Nothing to apologise for, Biff,' I said holding up my hands.

'I ain't apologising!' he corrected me, sharply. 'Just trying to tell you about it. Let's get that straight.'

'Straight,' I said, not wishing to pursue the subject one inch further.

'What the hell are we going to do, Kovachs?'

'Well, you can start by levelling with me.'

'What do you mean?'

'I mean telling me what you know about Johnny and Creel.'

'Goddamn you, Kovachs!'

'No atomic explosions, or I walk.'

Biff Lasky expelled a Gulliverian sigh as he swallowed his next intended verbal punch. 'Okay. Okay. So let's go over it.'

'Let's go over it, over some Brazil vapors.'

'What?'

'Coffee. Beppo makes an espresso that could grow hair on a chrome bumper.'

Biff Lasky had all the hair he needed and then some, but he agreed and we went back to Beppo's. He seemed a changed man once he began talking.

Johnny Scaduto, he told me, was interested in more than cleaning up the trucker's union. 'He wanted to get rid of the crooks in the industry, too. Johnny always said, it didn't make sense to reform the union if we didn't sweep the thieves out of the trucking industry as well.'

'Makes sense,' I interjected.

147

'Sure, it makes sense, but it ain't the union's problem to police the industry. If it directly affects the operation of the union, if it affects the workers, then I'm all for it. But Johnny was on a moral jag. To him it was a principle. He couldn't separate the two things. I argued about it with him a hundred times. Couldn't budge him an inch. But I respected his position. I always respected Johnny's opinion.'

Biff told me that Scaduto had been working for a long time to get the goods on Creel. A year or so ago he decided the best way to do that was from inside Creel's operation.

'Creel ain't no dummy,' said Biff. 'He was suspicious of Johnny at first. I mean with Johnny's reputation as an oppositionist and all. But Johnny was smoother than Chinese silk. He could talk the spots off a leopard, that's how good he was. It took six months, but Johnny worked his way into Creel's ring. This was strictly undercover stuff, Kovachs. Creel thought Johnny was his spy in the TDA. Nobody in the local but me knew what Johnny was up to and I don't know all of it. Johnny never told me exactly what he was doing with Creel. He only told me what he wanted me to know. Said that way we would both be protected. With the election coming up, Creel must have got scared. Maybe someone tipped him off that Johnny was playing him for a fall guy and was going to put him behind bars after we won the election. That's the way I figure it, Kovachs. Creel got scared. Maybe he had Johnny bumped off.'

'That a fact or a theory?'

'Well, I don't know anything about any argument Johnny had with Creel. Maybe he did, maybe he didn't. Either way, all the cards point to Creel, don't they?'

'What about the guy you throttled yesterday?'

'Packer? He's in with Creel up to his eyeballs. He's been on the take for years. If he thought Johnny was fixing to bust up Creel's operation, he'd have put on track shoes to make sure he was first in line to slit his throat.'

'So Packer could have killed Johnny?'

'Packer's a dumb sonofabitch, but he's too careful to have walked into that bowling alley with a gun in his pants. He has a whole barnful of goons who could have done the job for him.'

'Who else had a reason to kill Johnny?' I said, lighting a Chesterfield.

Biff raised one eyebrow. 'Who else?' he said. 'Ain't Creel and Packer enough? Maybe you think I killed Johnny.'

'Put it back on simmer, Biff. I'm just asking. What about the people at the bowling alley. A mug on Scaduto's team had a lot to say about what pals he and Johnny were, but was a whole lot more interested in rolling a 200 game.'

'Probably Ted Smiley. Just a dog face. He don't mean nothing.'

'Then there was Mabel Myers. She was Scaduto's girl, wasn't she?'

'Yeah, she used to be. They had been together for ten years before Johnny threw her over.'

'When was that?'

'A month ago. Maybe longer.'

'How convenient. And Hegan. I suppose he had a reason to kill Johnny Scaduto?'

'I don't know. Maybe he's not on the level, but I don't think he's got it in him to kill somebody. He comes on as a big militant at TDA meetings. Almost always took my side in any argument, but I don't like the man. He smells funny, if you know what I mean.'

I pushed my hat back on my head. 'Any more suspects? It's going to take Mickey Spillane to figure this one out.'

'The hell, you say!' Biff shouted, his large face turning the color of a beefsteak tomato. 'Creel and Lemmons are behind Johnny's murder. I don't care who actually pulled the trigger. Johnny's killing was political and Lemmons and Creel are the guilty ones!'

'That's fine, Biff, but how do you go about proving it. We need a lot more evidence than you've been able to come up with.'

'Bullshit, Kovachs! The hell with you and your bourgeois evidence. I don't want to try Creel and Lemmons in court.'

'Oh?'

149

'They could both beat the rap no matter how hard the evidence. The system is built for them to slip through. And what they can't get away with, they can buy their way out of. You should know that, for Chrissakes! Look, they've been breaking workers' bones and lining their pockets with cash they skimmed from union and company for years. Hell, Kovachs, you've been around. Crime *does* pay!'

I couldn't really put up an argument. Nobody in his right mind could.

'So, what do you do,' I said, 'if you don't take them to court?'

'The union can take care of them. The union when it's in the hands of the workers. That's the way. Christ Kovachs, you sound like Johnny. A damn bourgeois . . .' Biff Lasky caught himself in mid sentence.

'A what, Biff? A bourgeois what?'

'Aw, hell, Kovachs, it's nothing personal. It's just that we can't count on the courts and the government to clean our house. But that's none of your business. Your business is finding Johnny's killer.' Biff reached into his pants pocket and pulled out his billfold. He tossed a twenty dollar bill on the table. 'Here, I want to add my share to what the others gave you. Find Johnny's killer.'

'Right. Should be a cinch. Creel, Packer, Hegan, Mabel Myers, Lemmons, the mob. A real cinch.'

'Look, mister, I don't even know who the hell you are. You might be a pig spit for all I know. The election's only a couple days off. You got half that time to come up with Johnny's killer. If we don't have someone by then the TDA can kiss the election goodbye.'

'I'll do my best.'

'Do better! I'll see you here tomorrow at the same time.' Biff rose from his chair, tossed a dime on the table for the coffee and walked out of Beppo's without saying another word. I wanted to tell him the cappuccino was thirty cents, but I had something else on my mind.

150

8

A half hour later I left Beppo's. I crossed San Bruno and was halfway up the first block of Silliman when two raw-meat-eaters in leather jackets and dirty hair jumped out of the night and planted themselves in front of me. They were swinging large link chains. There were no watches on the other end. I turned around to try another direction, but two more pugs, bigger than the first two, were standing in my path flexing their brass-bound fists.

'Say, one of you fellas wouldn't happen to have change for a dollar, would you?' I said, for no apparent reason. They just grinned and made menacing sounds with their hardware. 'Was it something I said?' I asked, 'Or is this going to be another one of those random muggings we hear so much about these days?'

'Shut up, wiseguy,' said one of their number. In the next minute they were on me like a sweaty shirt. I took a brass fist to the kidneys that doubled me over like folded wash. Made me mad, it did. From my bent position, I rammed one of the chain-swingers. My head into his breadbasket. Then I straightened up and sent a hard right special-delivery to a face that would have embarrassed a bulldog. And that's all I remember. The next thing I knew, I was vaguely conscious and unmistakably sore. Very sore. Everywhere sore. Biff Lasky was bending over me.

'I see the goons got to you, Kovachs,' he said helping me to a sitting position.

When I was able to make words, I said, 'You here to prove your point or help me off the sidewalk?'

'Both,' he said, grinning slightly. He helped me to my feet and walked me wobbly to my car. When I had saved enough breath to speak again, I asked him why he'd come back looking for me.

'When I got to my place, I saw a couple of Lemmons' strongarms holding up lamposts. I figured if they were after me they might want a piece of you, too. I came back to warn you.'

I tried to smile, but my face wouldn't cooperate. 'Good thing you weren't Paul Revere or we'd still be a British colony.'

'You don't look so good, friend. Better get home and get some sleep.'

'Yes, mother. I'll call you tomorrow if I turn anything up.'

'You'd better, Kovachs.'

Biff dumped me behind the wheel of my Henry J and disappeared down the street. Strange guy, I thought, lighting a Chesterfield. A very strange guy.

9

I spent a good part of the morning trying to get out of bed. The pains demanded a lot of my time and nearly all of my attention. But I had work to do.

I called Hegan. He had no new information, but was quite liberal with the old when I asked him to review the Lasky-Scaduto friendship.

'Johnny and Biff,' he said, 'were friends long before I knew either one of them. But this election has put a strain on everybody.'

'Meaning?'

'Meaning Johnny and Biff, being leaders of the movement, were constantly under a lot of pressure. Tempers have been real short the last few weeks. It was bound to happen sooner or later.'

'Don't keep me guessing, Hegan. What was bound to happen?'

'Johnny and Biff. They had a row at the last big TDA meeting. It was one of those heat of the moment things. You know how that is.'

'They had a fight?'

'Not a fight, really. I'm telling you this, Kovachs, so you don't get it wrong from somebody else.'

'So tell me.'

'You know how Biff is. He lost his head and took a poke at Johnny. Not that Johnny didn't deserve it. He was saying some strange things. Upset a lot of people.'

'Strange things? Like what?'

'Like maybe the TDA should pull back and wait until the next election to go after Creel and Lemmons. He said we should take a low profile until after the Congressional Committee completed its investigation.'

'I could see where that would get Biff steamed.'

'It steamed a lot of us, including me, I don't mind telling you. Biff accused Johnny of going soft on Creel and the corruption in the union. A lot of us felt Biff was right and that Johnny was throwing our chances to win the election. But you got to understand, Johnny was a more popular guy than Biff and a whole lot better when it came to speaking. By the end of the meeting, if we had taken a vote, Johnny would have carried the majority.'

'What are you driving at, Hegan? That Biff Lasky and Scaduto had become enemies?'

'Just the opposite, Kovachs. I want you to get it straight. You know how rumors make mountains out of molehills. Sure, Biff and Johnny had an argument. They had a lot of differences. But, hell, that's the nature of union politics. Specially considering Biff. He's so damn emotional. I'm telling you all this so you don't go making more out of this thing than there really is.'

'Yeah, Hegan, thanks. A person who didn't know better

might think Lasky had a pretty good motive to bump off Scaduto wouldn't they?'

'That's why I'm trying to set you straight. Biff's a hothead. That's no secret. And this election has led him to do some foolish things. But he's no murderer, Kovachs. You get me?'

'Yeah. I get you. A pretty loyal Lasky supporter, aren't you, Hegan?'

'I've got nothing to hide. Like I told you, he's a good man for the union.'

'Yeah, so you told me. Who else have you been setting straight about Biff Lasky?'

'Well, the police questioned me and I told them the same thing I'm telling you. I'm no fink, Kovachs, but I felt they'd be more likely to leave Biff alone if they got the story straight the first time.'

Hegan was a study in good intentions. I thanked him for his information and told him to get back to me if he heard anything new. I hung up the phone and walked around my flat for a couple of minutes. Then I grabbed my coat and got my hat and went looking for the sunny side of the street. I hoped Mabel Myers lived there.

10

Mabel Myers lived in a Mission district flat near Dolores Park. A faint smile broke through the red, chapped face, and pink, water-logged eyes that greeted me at the door. She said she had been crying, but she didn't have to.

'It's nice to see you again, Mr Kovachs,' she said. 'Won't you please come in?'

I stepped inside and removed my skimmer. She motioned me into her living room and pointed to a large mohair easy

154

chair. 'Please sit down. I'll make some tea.' Before I could refuse, she disappeared into the kitchen. I followed her through the hall and sat down at the kitchen table covered with bright blue oil cloth. She didn't seem to mind.

'Mr Kovachs,' she said stiffly, 'if you need more money I can give you . . .'

I held up my hand. 'I can always use more money, but I didn't come here for that. I'm here to report what I've found and to ask you some questions.'

The tea kettle began whistling about the time I finished my brief report. Mabel Myers poured hot water into a bright red fiesta-ware pot and a few minutes later into two matching cups.

My report finished and the tea poured, I got right to the point. 'You and Johnny Scaduto broke up recently. Why?'

Her hand trembled as she hurriedly returned her cup from mouth to saucer. 'Really, Mr Kovachs, I don't think that is any of your business,' she said sternly.

'Murder is my business. Miss Myers. And we're talking about murder.'

'But I don't see. . . .'

'I don't either, but it may all come together if I have all the pieces. So, I ask you again, Miss Myers, why did you and Johnny Scaduto call it quits?'

Mabel Myers fidgeted nervously with a teaspoon as she spoke. Her eyes were in her tea cup. 'It was nothing, really, Mr Kovachs. Johnny and I had been together for quite a few years and we just decided it was time for a change.'

'I think it's time for the truth, Miss Myers. If this is painful, I can understand. But I've got to insist that you level with me.'

Mabel Myers stopped playing with her teaspoon. She raised her eyes from the bottom of her cup and fired a pair of angry coal-like pupils into my eyes. 'Biff Lasky split us up, if you must know. I wanted to marry Johnny. I had wanted to marry him for a long time, but Biff Lasky was always there to prevent it. He just couldn't stand anyone competing for Johnny's attention. He always used to tell

155

Johnny that the union was more important than our personal lives. He held that over Johnny's head like a club.

'Believe me, Mr Kovachs, I would never take Johnny away from his union work. I was in the union myself and worked for the TDA since the day it started. That's the funny part, isn't it? But Biff never let up on Johnny. He poisoned Johnny against me and I will never forgive him for that.'

She stopped for a moment. Her eyes drifting from mine and floating out the kitchen window. They were teary when they returned.

'About three months ago,' she continued, 'I told Johnny I wanted to get married and I wasn't going to wait any longer. I told him I wanted children. He knew that. Maybe that scared him. But I told him I wanted to work with him in the union. There was never any question about that.'

'He turned you down?'

'He said we'd have to wait until after the election. I refused.' Her wandering eyes returned to mine. 'I wasn't being impossible, Mr Kovachs. I had to take a stand. If I waited until after the election, there would be something else to postpone the marriage. It wasn't the first time Johnny had told me to wait.'

'So that was it? You walked out?'

'No, but things were never the same between us after that. Johnny began to sound more and more like Biff Lasky every day. Then, all of a sudden, he stopped talking about the union and the election altogether.'

'Why was that?'

'I can't really say, because I saw less and less of him. Then, about a month ago, we stopped seeing each other altogether except for the nights we bowled league. And then we didn't talk much.'

'That was strange, wasn't it? Was there another woman?'

'I don't know. Johnny cut me out of his life with no explanation. I guess that's what it means, though, doesn't it?'

'It might.'

'I mean, a man you've been with for more than ten years,

a man you love just walks out of your life v
What am I supposed to believe, Mr Kovachs
'You're bitter about the way things turned c
Miss Myers?'
Mabel Myers turned her head away and beg
'Well, how do you think I'm supposed to feel?' she said
chokingly. 'How would you feel, Mr Kovachs, if your girl
walked out on you? Huh, Mr Kovachs? Tell me that. How
would you feel?'
'I might feel like killing her.'
Mabel Myers froze. Her eyes betrayed shock. She got up
from her chair. 'You'd better leave now, Mr Kovachs.'
'I've got a few more things I'd . . .'
'Now, Mr Kovachs!'
She pointed a very stiff finger toward her front door. I had
gotten under her skin. Maybe it was just the emotional heat
of a woman thrown over that was booting me out of her
house. Then again, it could have been a whole lot more. But
then wasn't the time to find out. I put on my hat and beat
a respectable retreat from Mabel Myers' Mission district flat.

11

Bernal Hill was a first-round knockout during the winter
months. Green as Anne Sheridan's eyes and just as
seductive. I took a spin around the loop road on the way
home. I pulled off the pavement on the south side of the hill
just to take a gander while I sorted things out in my head.
I popped a lifesaver in my mouth and lit up a Chesterfield.
I got out of my car and propped my arms and chin on the
roof and stared out over Visitacion Valley, beyond McLaren
Park to San Bruno Mountain. The spiny-ridged hill stretched

n the Bay to Daly City. It was a soft, dull green and
ooked like a gigantic prehistoric reptile climbing out of the
sea. Sometimes my mind plays tricks on me. A mountain
looking like a dinosaur I could live with. The murder of a
man was something else.

I crossed the road and scrambled up the crumbly chert
rockslide to the little trail system that rings the hill. During
the next twenty-five minutes I thought about the Scaduto
killing and how everybody – Creel, Packer, Hegan, Lasky
and Mabel Myers had a reason to murder him.

By the time I had circled the hill, the only thing I had come
up with was mud on my shoes. That and a nagging feeling
that Biff Lasky still had some levelling to do.

I scraped the mud from my shoes and returned to the car.
I decided to stop home for some coffee and a couple of phone
calls. After all, I was in the neighborhood.

12

I walked through the front door to my flat and flipped my
hat on the desk. The hairs in my nose grew stiff even before
my eyes told me I had company. It was Lt. Flange and one of
his monkeys in baggy serge. They were making themselves at
home in the only two chairs in the place.

'Lt. Flange,' I said, shaking a Chesterfield from an open
pack on the desk. 'If I'd have known you were coming, I
would have baked a cake.'

Flange stood up. 'Save it, Kovachs. This ain't exactly a
social call.'

'Then you'll understand about the cake.'

'Wise up, Kovachs. We got some questions to ask you.'

'You know me, Flange, always ready to assist the city's finest. Shoot. I mean, what's on your mind, if you'll pardon the expression.'

'Where's Biff Lasky?'

'Who?'

'Don't be a dope, Kovachs. We know you and Lasky have been seeing a lot of each other lately.'

'It's nothing serious, Flange. He hasn't even taken me home to meet his mother yet.'

Something I said set off Flange's partner. He stood up and jerked a finger at me. 'We got ways to make you talk, wise guy.' He cracked his knuckles and started toward me. He was shorter than most men, but he had the neck of a mule and a face that looked like the bad side of town.

'Flange, call off your gorilla or I'll report you to the Humane Society.'

Flange stepped between me and his advancing partner. 'Forget it, Kolodny.' Kolodny stopped. He curled his lip at me and turned away.

'Thanks, Flange. I think you saved my life.'

'I'll come right to the point, Kovachs. We've got an arrest warrant for Lasky.'

'Oh!'

'Murder one. He killed his buddy. A trucker named Scaduto.'

'You're off your rocker, Flange. This is a political killing. Scaduto and Lasky were on the same side. Even you should know that. You should be looking for a couple of customers called Creel and Packer.'

'You telling me my job, Kovachs?'

'Not me, Flange. If I were in a position to tell you your job, I'd have you start by shooting yourself in the foot and then work your way upward.'

'Where's Lasky, Kovachs?'

'Who put you on to Lasky, Flange? Lemmons? Creel? Even you should smell a frame. I'm telling you, Creel and Packer. One runs a hot cargo ring at Scaparelli's and the other is a blaster for Lemmons. There's where you'll find Scaduto's killers.'

'How 'bout we run you downtown, Kovachs?'

'On what charge?'

'Obstruction of justice. Accessory to murder, before, during and after the fact. And that's just for starters.'

Kolodny started toward me again. 'You want me to put the cuffs on him, Lt.?' he said through an opening at the corner of his mouth.

'What'll it be, tough guy. Cooperation or the can?'

'You can put your cooperation in the can and flush it, Flange. I'm not going to help you frame Biff Lasky. Even if I knew where he was, I wouldn't tell you.'

'Union brothers, eh? Solidarity forever and all that crap. Most your labor guys are wearing red rompers under the overalls as far as I'm concerned. If it were up to me, I'd take all of them, including you, and put them on a boat and send it to Russia. That's what I'd do. You guys make me sick.'

'Good. Guys like us are supposed to make guys like you sick. If you get sick enough, maybe you'll croak.'

Kolodny grabbed me by the arm and twisted it behind my back. He jerked it up, stopping just this side of snapping it off at the shoulder. 'Want me to mess him up a little, Lt.?' he asked hopefully.

'Nah, let him go.'

'Let'm go? But you said . . .'

'I said let him go!'

Kolodny released his grip on my arm. My flipper dangled at my side like a Chinese wind chime. I rubbed life back into it.

Flange wasn't through with me. 'Kovachs,' he said, 'there's only one reason I'm not running you in this time. I got orders to bring in Lasky this afternoon. I can't be wasting my time filling out police reports with a small time nothing like you. Come on Kolodny, we've got work to do.' Flange and his sidekick hitched up their pants and started for the door.

'Flange!' I called out.

The Lt. turned and growled, 'Yeah?'

160

'What've you got on Lasky, really?'

Flange smiled. 'Something just as good as the murder weapon with his prints on it.'

In a second, the two cops were gone. I opened the windows to let in some fresh air.

I went to the kitchen to boil some water for coffee. I lit a smoke, pulled up a kitchen chair and sat sipping, smoking and staring at a picture postcard I received the other day from a friend in France. It was Arles, the place in France. That's the place where Van Gogh painted his masterpieces. Many years ago I read Irving Stone's biography of the Dutch painter and I could remember his description of Arles – 'A hot lemon yellow sun, a cobalt sky and furrowed earth that looked purple in the late afternoon.' I wished I was there.

But I wasn't – I was here. And I could feel the frame around Biff Lasky getting tighter and tighter. I felt pretty hopeless to do anything about it.

13

At 6.00 I climbed into my Henry J and headed for Beppo's for my meeting with Biff Lasky. I wasn't looking forward to telling him I hadn't turned up anything significant during the past twenty-four hours. What's more, I had to tell him, if the cops hadn't already nabbed him, that he was at the top of their hit parade of murder suspects.

I got to Beppo's ten minutes later. Biff wasn't there. Beppo said he'd stopped by a half hour before and gave him a message to give to me. Beppo handed me a piece of folded paper. On it was an address and a note that said only 'Meet me there.'

Twenty minutes later I was in the parking lot of the Paradise Lanes. That's where Biff wanted me to meet him. I went inside and scanned the alleys. Biff was bowling alone on number 18. I walked over. He was standing with his back to me waiting for his ball at the ball return rack.

'Biff!' I said above the rumble of rolling ebony and flying wood.

He turned around and smiled. 'Kovachs! Get yourself a ball and pair of shoes.'

'Are you nuts? This is no time to be bowling.'

Biff picked up his ball from the rack and started for his mark on the alley. 'I said get a ball and a pair of shoes. We can talk while we bowl.'

'The cops are after you, man! Don't you know that?'

'Yeah, but I'm on a hot streak right now. So get your ball and shoes, willya?'

There was no point in arguing with him. The man wants to bowl, so we bowl. I went up to the lane manager's desk and traded a dime for a pair of red and green size ten shoes. It took me a couple more minutes to find the right ball. I like a wide spread grip with a tight thumb hole. Anything else just won't do.

I joined Biff Lasky on number 18. He had just completed his second game – a 183. He wasn't happy. 'I blew a 9–10 pickup in the eighth,' he said. 'Coulda had me a 200 game. Kovachs, you go. I already started with a strike. Take a practice ball if you want.

I waved my hand indicating I was ready to bowl for keeps. I picked up the ball, found my mark on the alley and began my four-step delivery. I pitched the ball slightly to the right of the center diamond at the foul line. I didn't know what kind of a hook I would have so I played it cautious.

The ball didn't hook at all and slid badly out of the pocket. I knocked down three pins.

'I thought you was a bowler,' Biff shouted at me. He smiled slightly. I shrugged my shoulders. I dried my hands on the towel hanging on a ring at the rear of the ball return while waiting for my ball to come back. A moment later I picked

162

it up and returned to my spot. This time I allowed for the lack of hook and drove the big black marble squarely into the pocket of the remaining pins scattering them every whichway.

'Good pickup,' said Biff, rising from his seat at the scoring table and stepping into the alley. He pulled his ball from the return and marched up to his mark. He took a quick three-step approach and pitched the ball about five feet down the alley. It hung near the gutter for the first third of its journey. Then it twisted and spun like a gyroscope back toward the middle of the lane. The ball picked up speed as it bore in on the 1–3 pocket. It sounded like a giant turbine at the Bonneville Dam. Then, as if guided by radar, the ball plowed into the small forest of painted wood. It was a direct hit and all ten pins exploded.

Biff made a jerking motion with his right arm as if he were pulling a bus cord. He glided backward a step or two and turned toward me. 'There's number two,' he said.

We barely exchanged a word during the next three frames. Biff had strung together four strikes. I had a spare, two strikes and an open. When he left the ten pin standing on his first ball in the fifth, he stomped back to the scoring table where I was sitting and gave it an angry pound with his fist.

He picked up the spare on his second ball. On his way back to sit down he stopped and looked me in the eye. 'You got Johnny's killer?' he said.

I turned away and walked to the ball return to dry my bowling hand. 'Biff,' I said, 'the cops are after you. They've got a warrant for your arrest. Everyone from Mabel Myers to Butch Hegan thinks you killed Johnny. And you're bowling like it's your regular league night. What gives?'

Biff shook a Camel from a pack he kept in his shirt pocket. He lit it and momentarily disappeared behind a swirl of rising smoke. 'I'm relaxing, Kovachs. Following doctor's orders you know.'

'What doctor?' I snapped.

'Well, you for one. You're always trying to put the brakes

on me. I'm just taking your advice, that's all. Now go on and bowl.'

I had a good reason for missing the five pin on my second ball. To begin with, it's one of my toughest pickups. Right in the middle of the alley – all alone, so vulnerable, so obvious. A sitting duck. I always go through something psychological when facing that fat, solitary, defenseless pin, with sixteen pounds of round, black heaviness in my hand. I lose my concentration. This time, however, it was Biff Lasky that was throwing my concentration off. He was beginning to get me as steamed as a pitcher of Anchor Beer.

By the seventh frame both Biff Lasky's game and my patience were coming apart. His first ball hit the head pin dead on, leaving the 6,7,9 and 10 pins standing – the railroad split. On his second ball he settled for two of the four pins. It was his first open frame of the game. He walked back and sat down in the chair at the scoring table. He was angry.

'Damn!' he said. 'I didn't need that split.' He looked at the score sheet. 'Christ!' he said, I'll have to strike out to get a 241. My all time best is 240. The pressure's really on, now, Kovachs,' he said, rubbing his hands together.

I slammed the fat, red scoring pencil in the tray above the scoring sheet. 'I'm not bowling another frame until you tell me what's going on.'

Biff lit another cigarette. 'Okay! Okay! Cool off, willya? I got the whole thing figured out, Kovachs. Here's the scoop. Yeah, I know the cops are after me. I got a tip from a pal and have been lamming it since this morning. And I've been doing a little detective work on my own. Figured I had to. You've come up with nothing but zeros since you started.'

I have a pretty tough hide and am not easy to insult. Besides, he was right. I asked him about his new career as a sleuth.

'Look, I've been tagged as the fall guy since way before Johnny took that slug. I mean Creel and Lemmons have been trying to knock me and Johnny out since we started the TDA. They couldn't do it by the book so they tried the divide and conquer strategy. It's an old story, Kovachs. You and me both know it chapter and verse.'

I lit a Chesterfield. 'I need some concrete to make a drive-way, Biff. All you've given me is the hole in the ground. We need name, motives, witnesses. That's what's going to get you out from under this frame.'

'That's what I'm trying to tell you, Kovachs. I know who killed Johnny.'

'Who?'

'Hegan.'

'Hegan?'

'Yeah, Hegan. You remember me telling you how I didn't trust him? Well, I did some checking on him this morning with a couple of pals of mine who work on the docks. You know where Hegan drew a paycheck before he started pushing a rig?'

I shook my head. Biff Lasky paused to light another Camel. The hum of black balls rumbling down waxed wood floors sounding like a squadron of B-29s looking for Dresden filled my ears.

Biff Lasky continued. 'I'll tell you where. He was a docker on the east coast. Only he wasn't no real longshoreman. He was a plant. A government spy to finger brothers. He was working for that Congressional Committee that is trying to bust the unions. They say they are going after the racketeers, but don't you believe it.'

'How do you know Hegan is mixed up in that?'

'I'm coming to that part, Kovachs. Hegan's the guy who called me from the bowling alley to tell me Johnny had been shot. Right away, I was suspicious. I asked myself, what was Hegan doing at the bowling alley? It's night and he's supposed to be at work.'

'Maybe he took the day off.'

'Okay. But what was he doing here at the Paradise? He's not in the league and I know for a fact he doesn't bowl. In fact, he hates it. Johnny asked him a couple times to bowl with us and he always said no.'

'That's not enough to pin a murder on the guy.'

165

'It all fits, Kovachs. Don't you see? The feds are trying to bust the unions – this Kefauver Committee – saying to the press they are trying to clean out underworld influences from organised labor. That's just half of the story. They might indict a couple hoods, but what they really want is to put the unions under government control.'

'I've heard something along those lines.'

'It's as clear as the callouses on my hands. If they round up too many mafiosi in certain unions, who's going to be left in charge? *Us!* That's who. And you can be sure they don't want the unions to be in the hands of a bunch of reds. So they're going after us, too.'

I nodded. Biff was making sense. Political sense. And if Hegan was who Biff Lasky said he was, he was better at spinning cobwebs than a card-carrying spider.

'It's perfect, Kovachs, don't you see? The Feds hire a fink like Hegan. The fink kills a militant oppositionist and sets up another – namely me – to be the fall guy. Then the government steps in under the smokescreen to clean out organised crime and puts the local in trusteeship under hand-picked control. Neat as a goddamn pin, don't you think? It's the godamnedest plot to destroy trade unionism they've ever dreamed up.'

Biff smiled and turned away from me. He walked up to the ball return, picked up his ball, moved to his spot, took his three steps and pitched his ball down the alley. Four seconds later, ten pins lay creamed all over the lane.

He stood at the foul line a moment admiring the destruction. I called out to him. 'Biff, how are you going to prove this? If Hegan is a fed, he is not likely to go blabbing to you or anyone else that he committed murder.'

'Don't worry, Kovachs, he'll be here in ten minutes,' he said turning toward me. 'We'll shake the sonofabitch down. Right here on number 18. Right on the spot where he killed Johnny.'

Biff and I traded places on the alley. I bent over to pick up my ball. 'How do you know he'll show up? You said he hates bowling alleys.'

166

'He'll show, alright. Don't worry about that. I called him before I came here and told him I knew who Johnny's killer was and I wanted him to come over and help me set a trap to catch him.'

'He went for it?'

'Hegan doesn't know I'm on to him. He thinks he's done a con job on me by all the time supporting me at meetings. Well, he'll be here and he'll be in for a big surprise. That's for sure.'

I stepped up to my mark and took my approach. I let fly with a hard one. The ball slid past the 1–3 pocket, crossing over the head pin and crashing into the Brooklyn side pocket. Ten dead sticks lay spinning in the gutter just the same.

'Nice ball, Kovachs,' Biff said, jumping up to take his turn. 'You an' me are going down to the wire in this one.'

'Yeah,' I said. 'Looks like you're up by only eight pins.'

Biff walked past me on his way to the ball return. He turned his head and spoke before I reached the scoring table. 'You carrying, Kovachs?'

'Carrying what?'

'A piece, man,' he said, patting the front pocket of his pants. 'This guy's a government fink who's killed at least one man. Don't think he won't come in here packing a rod.'

I gulped. I wasn't carrying anything other than a handkerchief, my car keys, some loose change and a very thin wallet.

Biff took down all ten pins again for his second strike in a row. He walked past me on my way to the ball return. 'Don't worry, Kovachs,' he said. 'It's just for insurance. You know me, I'm more likely to break his neck than fill him full of lead.'

'Sorry, but I'm not consoled,' I said picking up my ball and moving to my spot.

'Don't worry. As long as he don't try any funny stuff, I'm not going to turn out his lights. Hegan's my way out of this thing, you know.'

My legs felt like they were made out of Jack cheese as I stepped up to my spot. But I had a three-strike 'turkey' going for me and was shooting for a fourth. My ball was working like clockwork and hit the pocket dead center. Maybe too dead center. The pins went flying so fast they left the 7 pin standing. But I had great luck. Another pin ricocheted off the opposite alley wall, bounced across the lane and knocked the 7 pin into the gutter. I yelled out loud.

'You sure know how to keep the pressure on a guy, Kovachs,' Biff said walking to the ball return. 'It looks like I'm going to have to strike out to beat you.' He looked at his watch. 'Looks like we'll just about have time to finish before Hegan shows up.'

Biff dried his right hand on the house towel before picking up his ball. He found his mark and blew on his thumb before sticking his fingers into the ball. Then, like a perfectly timed V-8 engine, made his approach and released the ball. It was almost automatic, the effortless way it found the 1–3 pocket and scattered all the pins. He made the cord-pulling motion with his right arm.

'That's one!' he said, smiling. He then repeated the entire procedure. 'That's two!' he shouted. He stepped up to the towel and pulled on it nervously. He got his ball and stepped up to his mark. He glided to the foul line as smoothly as three ounces of Neat's Foot Oil and launched his ball down the alley. It was all over before any contact was made. The pins exploded as if the pin boy had set off a dynamite charge.

Biff Lasky jumped in the air. 'Yahee! A 241! That's my all-time high game! Damn! I had my ball working that alley, didn't I?'

I got up from the scorer's table to shake his hand. 'Great game, Biff. You're a real pro.'

Biff blushed slightly. 'Aw, go on 'n bowl, willya.'

I walked up to the towel ring and pulled at it with my right hand. Both my mitts were wringing wet and it wasn't from the tension produced by stringing together four strikes. I surveyed the lanes looking for a sign of Butch Hegan. I didn't like the way I felt. Biff was too calm and collected and I had allowed my attention to be sucked into my game. But there was nothing to do but go for it – my fifth strike.

I toed my mark, lowered the ball to my waist and lurched

forward. One, two, three, four steps, release. The ball hit its spot on the wood and began twisting down the alley toward the pocket. Smack! A perfect hit. The pins flew, but when their death dance was completed, the five pin stood alone, erect in the center of the lane, untouched, defiant. My heart sank. I fell to my knees as if praying to an angry god. But it didn't help. I stood up and walked back to dry my hand, retrieve my ball and go for the spare.

As I bent over to get my ball I saw Hegan on the level above the lanes. He was moving furtively toward number 18, toward Biff who sat with his back to him. Hegan was carrying a gun in his right hand.

'Biff!' I called out. 'Hegan! Behind you! He's got a gun!'

In the next instant, Biff dove from the chair at the scorer's table to the floor. 'Get down!' he said, pulling his gun from his pocket. I crouched alongside the ball return. I looked up to see Lt. Flange and a couple uniformed cops join Hegan at the wall overlooking our alley.

'Flange!' I shouted. 'Hegan's your killer! We can prove it! Get him before somebody gets hurt!'

'Stay out of this, Kovachs!' Flange yelled back. 'We're here for Lasky and I don't care how we take him.'

The commotion had alerted the bowlers on the nearby alleys that something other than bowling was taking place. They scattered and took cover behind benches, ball racks, anything that would protect them from flying lead without totally giving up their ringside seats to the impending shootout.

'Biff!' I shouted. 'The place is lousy with cops. Give it up!' Before he could answer, Hegan drew a bead and fired at the squatting union militant. Biff Lasky jumped up and squeezed off two rounds. One hit Hegan in the shoulder. The other plowed into a bowling ball in one of the house racks. Flange and the other cops began filling the air with lead.

Biff dropped to the floor and took cover. He turned to me. 'This is it, Kovachs!' he yelled. 'They don't want to take any prisoners!'

I screamed at Flange at the top of my voice to call off the

169

gunplay. A slug in the ball return an inch from my head was his answer.

While Biff Lasky was trading shots with Flange and his blasters, Hegan, who had momentarily disappeared, re-surfaced down on alley 19. He had a clear shot to Biff's blind side. He drew careful aim.

'Biff!' I shouted. 'Behind you!' I picked up a bowling ball from the return and heaved it in Hegan's direction. But before it left my hand, Hegan fired once. He hit his mark. Biff spun around, rose to one knee, looked at me curiously, began to take a step toward me and collapsed at the edge of the alley.

I rushed to where he lay. I took his head in my hands. 'Kovachs,' he said, 'they got me. The bastards got me.'

'Don't talk, Biff.' I turned toward Flange, who was approaching us. 'Flange! Call a goddamn ambulance!' He ignored me and continued walking to where Biff Lasky was lying in a puddle of his own blood.

Biff saw him out of his dimming eyes. 'Flange,' he said weakly, 'do me a favor and give me a couple minutes with Kovachs.'

Flange, who still had his gun pointed at the fallen unionist, looked down at him. 'Well, I guess you ain't going nowhere,' he said. He turned and walked over to Hegan, who was sitting on the bench on 19, nursing his wounds.

'Kovachs,' Biff said, in a raspy voice. 'I got something I want to say. So you'll know. It'll probably come out anyway.'

'Easy, Biff, easy. The ambulance is on the way.'

'Forget the goddamn ambulance. I killed Johnny.'

'What?'

'You heard me. Hegan or maybe one of his flunkies pulled the trigger, but it might as well have been me.'

'Biff, what are you talking about?'

'Johnny had gotten in over his head with Creel. It happens. I don't know how Creel did it, Kovachs, but he trapped Johnny. Hegan knew about it and set Johnny up. Blackmail, threats, bribes, I don't know that part. But they forced Johnny to sell out the TDA. He was going to pull out of the election. I just couldn't let him do that, Kovachs. Not after all we had worked for.'

Biff coughed weakly and asked me for a smoke. I lit one of my Chesterfields and placed it in his mouth. He took a drag and continued talking.

'I argued it out with him for a solid month. Even had a fight at our last TDA meeting. I pleaded with him, Kovachs. As a friend, as a comrade. For old time's sake, for the future of the union. Nothing would budge him. He said it would take more time to get the goods on Creel and didn't want to queer things, but I knew that he had got locked into something criminal and couldn't get out. He just got in over his head.'

Biff coughed again. A trickle of blood squeezed out the corner of his mouth. His face had turned the color of a mackerel.

'How does Hegan fit into this?' I asked.

'Like I said, Hegan had always been real buddy-buddy with me. He took me out drinking after the meeting I took a poke at Johnny. Hegan kept feeding me drinks and I kept getting madder and madder at Johnny and what he was doing to the TDA. I was almost out of my head, Kovachs. My best friend turning rat and pulling the rug from under the rank-and-file. Hegan said he could fix Johnny if I gave him the word. He never said how he was going to fix him, but I knew what he had in mind, Kovachs. I knew exactly what he had in mind. I must've been out of my head because I said "go ahead and fix the fink sonofabitch". That's what I said, Kovachs. I signed Johnny's death warrant. I put that bullet in his back.'

'Like you said, Biff, you were out of your head. You weren't responsible for what you said.'

Biff took another drag off the cigarette. 'Hegan called yesterday and played me a tape recording he made that night. He told me who he was and said he was going to put me away unless I pulled out of the election. I told him to shove it. Nobody pushes Biff Lasky around without a scrap. So I arranged this little shooting party. I figured one or both of us was going to boot hill and anyway it come out, it was better than spending the rest of my life behind bars. Sorry I had to get you mixed up in it, Kovachs.'

Biffs voice trailed off. He coughed again. His eyes rolled once and he was gone.

Lt. Flange tapped me on the shoulder. 'Did he croak yet?'

I turned around and looked up at him. 'Flange, he's dead, thanks to you and your gunmen.'

'Hold on, Kovachs. He started firing first. We got witnesses.'

I laid Biff Laskey's head down on the alley and got to my feet. The ambulance attendants had arrived. 'Don't feed me that crap, Flange. You came in here to execute him.'

'Hey, he was a murderer. Killed his buddy.'

'You're the murderer. You and Hegan.'

'You looking for a ride downtown, smart guy? I could slap an accessory charge on you. It'd be real easy.'

Hegan, who had been given first aid for his shoulder wound, walked over to look at the body. 'Good work, Lt.,' he said. 'We were lucky. Lasky is a pretty tough customer. Anyone who would gun down his best friend.'

'You make me laugh, Hegan,' I said. 'And my skin crawl.'

'What've you got to be sore about, Kovachs? Are you opposed to cleaning up the criminal element in the labor unions?'

'Biff Lasky was no criminal and you know it. You set him up for this. You got to Scaduto with your talk about giving him government help to clean up the industry and pushed him into Creel's outfit. Then you threatened to send him to the joint along with Creel if he didn't bring down Lasky and the TDA.'

Hegan smirked. 'You're nuts, Kovachs.'

'Maybe. But not about this. Then you began feeding Biff stories about how Scaduto sold out the TDA. You drove a wedge between them. You sabotaged the TDA and pushed Lasky to the wall, suckering him into believing he ordered Scaduto's killing.' I turned to Flange. 'You looking for an

172

accessory, Flange? You got one. United States government agent Hegan!'

Hegan put an arm on Flange's shoulder. 'Let's go downtown, Lt.,' he said, 'and file our reports. I think we'll both be in line for a commendation.'

Flange looked at me and smiled. 'Yeah, let's get out of here. And Kovachs. About your story. Tell it to Gus Hall.' Both he and Hegan laughed out loud and walked away.

I stood by as ambulance attendants put Biff on a stretcher and carried him away. A dozen reporters were climbing up each others' backs to get something quotable from Flange and Hegan. Not to mention the photographers.

The papers would have a field day with this one. It would be reported as another internal union rivalry that ended in bloodshed. Another spike to drive into the ticker of the labor movement. Another feather in the cap of the forces of 'law and justice'.

Biff was right. He was right about the federal government trying to interfere with the trade union movement. Hegan was a textbook case. He sprung traps for both Johnny Scaduto and Biff Lasky. First, he set up Scaduto, counting on his streak of naivety that looked to the government to help clean up the trucking industry. Once Scaduto was ensnared in some illegal activity with Creel, Hegan owned him and that forced Biff's hand. Either swallow Scaduto's sabotage of the TDA election chances or take out Scaduto. Hegan gets Biff drunk and mad and in a moment of temper he gives in to Hegan's prodding that he can 'fix' Scaduto.

Then Hegan has Scaduto iced with Biff nailed dead-bang on a conspiracy or accessory charge. Nice and neat. 'Your government working for you' as they say. If Uncle Sammy were only half as competent when it comes to solving the real problems that are putting folks through hard times. But I gave up believing in the tooth fairy a long time ago.

I should have known Hegan was the key to the whole thing. I should have known that Biff was holding back on me, too. I should have known a lot of things that I didn't. But even if I had known, it wouldn't have changed things

173

much. I mean if the feds are determined to get you, it doesn't matter whether you've committed a crime or not, they'll get you. Biff knew what he was up against. He knew that Hegan would make what he had, weak as it was, stick like peanut butter. There was no way he would even consider fighting it out in the courts. No, the way Biff Lasky figured his chances, it was shoot or be shot; kill or be killed. Plus, there was a little matter of revenge. Hegan murdered, or had someone murder, his best friend. And even though his best friend had turned rat, I'm sure Biff couldn't forget the twenty years they spent together building the workers' movement. Biff Lasky wasn't the kind of guy who would forget that. Even though he was in a tight spot he must have felt taking Hegan down with him would balance the books.

But it didn't work out that way. Hegan and Flange walk away heroes. The government and the police come out smelling like roses and the militants, guys like Biff Lasky and Johnny Scaduto, guys who spent their whole lives fighting crooks and corruption and wanted nothing more than to return their unions to the honest working stiffs, they get it in the back. They take the fall. Don't get me wrong, it doesn't always come out that way, but enough times so that it has become what might be called 'the American tradition'.

I sat on the bench on number 18 smoking a Chesterfield and staring at the spots of blood on the alley where Biff fell. I barely heard my name called. I looked up. It was Mabel Myers.

'I saw what happened, Mr Kovachs. I don't pretend to understand everything that has happened in the last two days, but when I saw that man Hegan walk into the bowling alley with the police, a lot of things began to make sense.'

'I don't know what you mean, Miss Myers.'

'Johnny told me about that man once. Said he was trouble, but not much more than that.'

'It might have helped if you had told me about it this afternoon.'

'I guess I didn't think it was important. I was bitter at both Johnny and Biff. That's why I came down here tonight. This

174

was the night Johnny and Biff bowled together. I knew Biff would be here.'

'What were you going to do, Miss Myers?'

'I, I don't know. I was going to have it out with Biff. But when I saw Hegan and the police start shooting at Biff, I realised that it was Hegan and not Biff that came between Johnny and me. It all just sort of fell into place, Mr Kovachs. I can't explain it other than I put what Johnny said about Hegan together with what I saw tonight. And I can bet that Hegan is responsible for a whole lot more than coming between Johnny and me. I can bet he is behind the political fights we've been having in the TDA.'

'Miss Myers, what you figured out in a minute had to be spelled out for me by a dying man. You've got it right. Just some details to fill in and I can do that for you. I hope you will tell people the real story behind Johnny's and Biff's death.'

'I'm going to do more than that, Mr Kovachs. The election is the day after tomorrow. I'm going to see to it that everyone in our local knows that the TDA is still running a slate and that we expect to win. Maybe not this time, Mr Kovachs, maybe not the next time either. But someday we will win.'

'I hope you do, Miss Myers. I really hope you do.'

Mabel Myers turned and walked out of the bowling alley. You had to admire her grit.

The lanes around number 18 had cleared out. In fact, all the alleys were strangely quiet. I looked down 18 and saw the five pin smack dab in the middle of the lane. I'd completely forgot it when the shooting started. Almost reflexively, I walked up to the ball return. I picked up my ball and walked to my spot. My mind was elsewhere. I went into my approach, hit my mark and watched the ball, starting near the lip of the gutter, twist back toward the center of the valley. The ball seemed to take forever making its way down the alley.

My eyes were glued on the five pin standing so defiantly in the middle of the lane. The ball bore in on it like a thousand pound bomb guided by radar. The ball reached its target,

175

but it slid by the pin, grazing it as it rolled off the end of the alley. For a moment the pin teetered back and forth on its small base like a metronome teasing gravity. But it didn't fall.

I walked away. I sat down on the bench and lit a Chesterfield. I changed my shoes, paid the tab for the lane and walked out of the Paradise Lanes. It would be a while before I would be able to return. A long while.